our dreams might align

our dreams

stories dana diehl

might align

JELLYFISH HIGHWAY PRESS | ATLANTA, GEORGIA

Cover and Layout Design by Justin Lawrence Daugherty

ISBN: 978-0-9967823-7-1

Published by Jellyfish Highway Press, Atlanta, GA 30312

For my family:
the collectors, the pilots, the explorers

contents

we know more 15

astronauts 25

burn 29

swallowed 47

swarm 51

animal skin 63

closer 67

stones 89

another time 93

to date a time traveler 97

the mother 105

a place without floors 107

once he was a man 117

girls prepare for the apocalypse 121

going mean 123

acknowledgments 143

The visions started a year before we met. Ashton dreams of an Earth with wide stretches of endless sand and uninterrupted sky. It's always the water that goes. He turns ponds into beds of dried seaweed and swimming holes into meteor craters. It's a firing of a synapse, a neuron interrupted, and suddenly we're in a dry world.

At the beginning of July, when the visions increase to once a week, twice a week, I drive Ashton to the hospital and wait for him in the parking lot. I work as a substitute, teaching ninth-grade Earth and Environment, but summer break started a month ago. I pace between the parking meters. I fill my meter with dimes. I say to myself: brain, Brussels, boxer, barracuda.

The next morning, Ashton invites me over for breakfast. His X-rays sit in a pile on the kitchen table next to the Cheerios box. After we eat, we go out into the back lawn so he can trace the white curve of his skull against the blue of the sky. All around us, half-formed fruits drop in the grass with a smell that reminds me of Fly Nap in biology labs. Ashton's fenced backyard is a forest of fruit trees, and I know he's planted, nurtured, each of them. I've seen him perched on a ladder, pruning back the branches, his body like a leaf curling in on itself. Ashton is six years younger than me, only twenty-five. I move my body closer to his, and my toes brush against fallen figs shaped like raindrops, skin rough and sticky. I imagine their fleshy fruit producing amylases, proteases, breaking down the tissue from the core out.

Ashton hands me the X-rays. I studied Human Anatomy in college, and it still looks so familiar. Six images, cross-sectioned and laid out next to each other like thin slices of melon. Here's the cerebellum, the temporal lobe. I touch the plastic, leaving a fingerprint on his brainstem. Ashton takes my hand and points it to a shadow pressed against his left occipital. He tells me it doesn't hurt, but he'll experience hallucinations, increasing as it grows.

"I won't blame you if you leave me," Ashton says, and I can tell he means it. He pushes hair out of his eyes. I reach for a low, arching branch of the apple tree.

"How long do you have?" I ask.

He shrugs. "Years. Maybe months. They don't know."

We've only been dating for half a year. I'm not attached to my job. We haven't been dating for long. It'd be easy to disappear, to move again. I think of a relationship with a set end date. A clock counting backward instead of forward. I let myself slip backward into the grass, soppy where he left the sprinkler on last night. I hold his brain up above me and watch as a robin flies through his temporal lobe.

It's early summer. The sun is out until ten, and I stay up late trying to imagine the world as Ashton sees it. The closest I can get is a story a friend told me about a road trip she took out west with other Biology students. One night they didn't stop to sleep. They just kept driving and driving until they reached the Thunder Basin Grassland. It was four in the morning, but they crouched in the gravel wide awake, watching the inky spread of Wyoming sky and listening to the wind in the grass.

we know more

Then, without planning it, they started to run. They shook prairie dog tunnels and galloped past the black silhouettes of slumbering elks. My friend swears the elk ran with them that night. She couldn't see them, but she could hear them, breath hot, hooves pounding through sagebrush. This is what it must be like to be Ashton, running through blackness, feeling that you could disappear at any minute.

Or maybe, it's like when I was thirteen, and I started keeping a diary in code, because my mother didn't believe in privacy for children. It was a code based on associations only I knew. When I stole a pair of pink pajama shorts from Victoria's Secret: windmills. When I skipped school, rode the bus to the ocean, and went swimming in my clothes: jellyfish. I started to see think in these codes as I experienced my life. My days transformed into something new.

When I show up on Ashton's doorstep the next morning and tell him I'll stay, he says he loves me. I don't say I love him back, but I wrap my arms around his waist and bend my neck so I can rest my head in the hollow of his chest. When he kisses me, he says he sees receding waves on the sidewalk. We spend the day sitting, our knees bent under our chins, in the foyer window, counting cars that go by and waiting for something to happen behind the windows of the houses. When I get bored, I take Ashton's skull between my palms and memorize its shape, feeling its contours, wondering what happened to make things go wrong underneath.

I feel like sharing. I show him I can name all the bones in his hand. I point to the crabapple tree in his backyard and explain how the water is sucked into the roots, how it travels through xylem tissue by adhesion and cohesion up the tree. He says he knows where to plant a seed by the feel of the ground. How cool it is, how easily the soil breaks apart between his thumb and forefinger.

I tell him I was engaged once, to a man who left me for Australia. Over summer break, I visited him in Sydney. It was the first time I left the country. He took me to a reservation some friends of his owned so I could see the marsupials he studied, koala bears that clung to my waist like fanny packs. At five one morning, he woke and drove me to the reservation so I could see the kangaroo give birth. It wasn't what I expected. A tiny fetus, naked and pink with swollen eye sockets, crawled up through the mother's fur and into the pouch. I saw the way he watched, and I knew I had lost him.

I tell Ashton this, and he cups his hand around the back of my neck, runs his fingers over the top vertebrae of my spine, like he's checking for something he's forgotten.

At the end of July, Ashton says he wants to see the meteor shower that he heard about on the news. That night, we turn off all the lights in his house and lie under blankets in the backyard. We can only see a few stars through the haze of streetlamps and porch lights, but Ashton insists that we stay outside.

The ground is warm, and the apples and clementines—small, forced to grow outside their time zone—and tiny pinecones hang in the branches above us.

I ask him, "Did you know you can tell what the meteor is made of by the color it burns?" and he shakes his head. I see the blink of a satellite, and I say, halfheartedly, that I think I saw a falling star.

"Ooh," Ashton says. "I saw it, too."

Soon, he's seeing shooting stars everywhere.

"Wow, April, look," he says. "I never knew, they have tails of water. Do you see?"

I stare at the sky, wishing I could, and see nothing. For an hour he describes it for me, a space full of stars propelled by fountains, planets rimmed in icy discs. The fruit hanging in the trees are moons.

When we go back inside, there's a bat fluttering around his ceiling fan, wings catching on the curtains and brushing against the rows of pots and pans hanging on the kitchen wall, making them clink together. It shadows through the house, gravitating toward the corners of the room, the hidden places. I ask Ashton if he left the back door open, and instead of answering he grabs a jacket from over the couch. He tosses it to me and grabs another from the hall closet. I imitate the way he holds it up over his head, clasping it by its arms, opening them like wings. Together, we approach the bat, which is trying to attach itself to the handrail. I can hear its claws making a raspy sound against the wood, polished and polyurethaned smooth. I close in, and the bat flies upward, then darts for the window. It smacks against the glass and falls, limp, onto the couch.

I approach the body. I've dissected bats like this. Seen the way the blood moves from their hearts to their wings. Fed them quarters of mangoes on a research trip to an animal sanctuary in New Mexico. The bat is covered in reddish brown fur and has a face like a fox. It's barely the size of my hand with my fingers outstretched. *Myotis lucifugus.*

"Look," I say, but Ashton won't touch it, won't leave his spot at the bottom of the stairs. I lift the tip of the bat's wing, which is crumpled closed like a black glove, and stretch it so I can feel the soft undersides, trace my pinky along the bones that connect the membrane.

"I think it's dead, Ash." Dark red blood runs out from the side of its mouth, and it is so still.

Ashton insists that it's just stunned. He asks me to put it out back, so it can fly away when it wakes up. I scoop it into my palms. I tell him I'll put it on the back patio, but once I'm outside, I run through the dark to the end of his yard to the compost heap. His shovel is leaning against a tree, and I dig into the rotting pile of orange peels and apple rinds and grass clippings until there's a hole as deep as the length of my forearm. I place the bat's body at the bottom and cover it up before going back inside.

August comes, and Ashton sees whirlpools in the sky. Water in the faucets turns to steam as it hits the air. He says a man has entered his dreams, tall and faceless. I wonder who it is, if it's someone from his past. Ashton rarely talks about the time before we were together.

Our relationship is contained in houses. I try to get him to go on a trip with me. I suggest we go camping or go to the beach. But he tells me he doesn't like to travel. I'm surprised to learn how many things he's afraid of. Open spaces. Storms. Distance. He tells me he likes to feel packed in, surrounded by other moving lives. He was happiest when he lived in an apartment. The voids in a house, in the spaces between the walls, in the attic, in the untouching houses, make him lonely.

I drive him to the doctor, and there he gets a new set of X-rays. In the waiting room, I explain what I learned in undergrad Biology, back when I still wanted to be a field sci-

entist, an explorer, a writer. On the microscopic level, everything is touching. Cells against cells. Cells against molecules.
I can be a block away from him, and if I wave my arm, I create
a chain reaction of movements that will touch him, even if he
can't feel it. Around Ashton, saying what's accurate doesn't
seem as important as saying what feels right.

A nurse calls Ashton's name, and I sit in the waiting
room for a while, watching the soap opera on the television.
It's mid-day, mid-week, and we're the only people there. I
move from one seat to the other, exploring the walled, win-
dowless space. When Ashton returns, he takes my hand. He
tells me the shadow's grown.

Back in his kitchen, we look at the X-rays together.
We place the images against the white of the counter. I can see
the dark of the tumor, pressing, filling. Ashton takes a breath,
grabs a Sharpie. I watch as he draws pictures in the spaces
between his lobes, pictures of serpents and tree roots that can
fit in the smallest gaps. He hands me a pen, and we cover the
dark space with smiley faces with their tongues sticking out.
I draw a stem at the top of his cerebellum so it looks like an
apple. Doodle myself biting a chunk out of it. When we're
done, Ashton hangs them with magnets on his fridge.

I watch Ashton's house from my car, knowing which room
he's in by which windows are lit up. I was supposed to have
left an hour ago. I only made it to the end of the street before
realizing I wasn't ready to go home yet. So I parked the car
by the curb, turned off the engines, and waited. When all of
the windows go dark, I slip out of the car and walk down the
street and into Ashton's backyard. The air is cool and the sky
is starry, and fruits, knocked off their trees in a rainstorm, lit-

ter the yard. I gather the clementines, which stand out bright and orange, into the space between my forearm and hip. Then, nervous, I sprint back to my car. When I get home I drop the fruits onto my living room carpet. I watch them roll across the floor, under the coffee table, against the vacuum cleaner.

I gather the clementines into a pile in my lap. I peel them apart with my fingernails, leaving a heap of orange skin at my feet. I break the fruit into quarters and hold them one by one on my tongue, tasting the sourness, testing to see how long I can hold them there. The tree didn't get enough sun for the fructose to form. I eat all but one clementine and place it on the stand beside my bed. Maybe I'll bring it to Ashton in the morning and tell him I bought it from the market. He'll eat the fruit slowly and gratefully. The sugar will tingle his fingers with warmth. The moment will be real despite the lie.

On the last day of summer, we sit cross-legged in his yard. Ashton has emptied his compost heap, spread it over his lawn and patches of garden. Frosts are coming, he says, and he's afraid the roots and seeds won't make it through the winter. He wants to give them this last boost, so now the yard swims with the smell of the oversweet. I wonder if he found the bat bones among the browned fruit peels, but if he did, he says nothing.

"Sunflowers, souvenirs, satellite," I say, leaning into the grass, pulling him down with me.

"Tidal, tsunami, tarot card," Ashton responds, joining my game.

I press my skull against his, feeling his hair brush against my bare forehead. I breathe in the smell of the leaves changing colors, chlorophyll drying in the shadows. I ask

we know more

Ashton to describe what it's like in those moments when the shadow in his brain takes over.

"It's like my skin disappears, and the world moves through me."

There are the sounds of a jet flying overhead and children playing in the yard next door. When Ashton speaks, I close my eyes and see a dry world. One in which we can walk, miles and miles, to the seafloor. I teach my Earth and Environment class that we know more about outer space than the deepest depths of the oceans. But in this world, Ashton and I will walk the tidal zones into the deep like land. We'll find old fishing boats, rusted lobster thatches, and fishing lines ringed in pearled oysters. We'll climb the Mid-Atlantic mountain range and see the corpse of a whale, starfish and colorful sand crabs crawling over its rotting flesh. We'll gaze into the Mariana trench, drop stones into its mouth, wait for their echoes. And it won't be a mystery anymore.

Things they never tell you when your husband leaves the planet:

It'll happen faster in real-life than it does on TV. *10, 9, 8…* A flash of orange and a shimmer of exhaust, and the shuttle is moving upward. The last time you saw your husband, he was waving down at you and your son from the shuttle ramp. Head shaved onion-raw for the trip, shiny under the camera lights. You tried to note hesitancy, regret, in his walk, but you couldn't find it, or you didn't look hard enough, and now he's gone. The shuttle is a white seagull sailing across the blue sky. The thunder of the engines and the firework-pop of the rockets roll over your viewing pad twenty seconds late, long after the shuttle disappeared.

For the first two weeks, you will keep the lights off in the evening, the shades drawn open. You say it's because the moths are always drawn to the house and tear their wings against the metal screens in their quest for the lamp bulbs, but you know this isn't the truth. You're trying to place your husband in the constellations. Trying to identify the moving light that is his. You'll wonder if you're looking at your husband now, tiny to the point of invisibility, a piece of space-dust in the black. You'll watch your son make shadow puppets against the living room wall with his flashlight and fists. Wait for your eyes to adjust to the sudden light.

You read this on Wikipedia: A person can survive in

space san-spacesuit for eight seconds. At nine seconds, the deoxygenated blood will reach the brain and the person will lose consciousness. At two minutes, blood boils from lack of air pressure, and organs burst. Wonder, does your husband know this? Wonder, if he did know, would he consider unlatching the shuttle door in the middle of the astronauts' fabricated night, stepping out into the black vacuum of space? Bodies suspend in cocoon-like sleepbags in the cabin around him. For those eight seconds, for the stars tangling in his hair and catching in the corner of his eyes like gnats, for the feeling of skin-to-space, might death be worth it?

You'll still see him, of course. It's the twenty-first century and distance slows a relationship, but doesn't sever it. Every week, you'll see your husband's face on Skype. His features are pixilated; when you hold the screen too close he dissolves into a hundred monochrome colors. Goodbye bike-accident scar. Goodbye grays hairs growing behind his ears. Somehow the cabin surrounding him looks more real than he does, a wall of buttons, white panels. Scan it for signs of familiarity, a little bit of you. *Hello, earthlings*, he'll say in a guttural, fake-robot voice. You notice how natural it sounds on him.

Three months will go by. You will start to feel like your body is disappearing. The mattress has conformed to your shape, it doesn't press against the angles of your hips anymore. In the close quarters of the shower, you breathe in your own breath, again and again. When was the last time you were touched? Take Polaroids of yourself, with the door locked, your kids downstairs watching television. Smile. Watch your figure form in the ink, tear it up just before it solidifies. Be afraid you're a ghost.

astronauts

When he returns to earth, six months later, he won't be able to walk. Day by day in anti-gravity, his muscles have deteriorated, his bones hollowed. He will lean against you. Feel his hip bones grinding against your own, smell his neck like a clean lab table. Ask him questions, you'll only know how to speak in questions. He'll answer with words like *incredible, amazing, breathtaking*. But you can't feel an adjective. At home, your husband sits in the rocker on the front porch, eyes closed, and for a month, this is the only place he'll sleep soundly. Admit to yourself that your body's learned to sleep in bed alone.

Your husband will always tell stories about his time in space. Before your son's first prom, he'll tell the date, who waits awkwardly in the foyer in a blue sweetheart dress, how it feels to break the thermosphere. When you have grandchildren, his stories will change for them to include moon monsters and deep space battles. As your husband talks of space, expect to remember an earlier time. Before you knew each other. Before you knew anyone other than your parents. A time when you could make-believe space travel in a cardboard box in the backyard. You so wanted the cardboard box to come to life, to take flight. Wanted it with every inch of your being. One time, a breeze caught you, tumbled the box and your body over the hill and into the vegetable garden. You emerge, and you're infuriated—not because you're bruised and tumbled, but because for a moment the spaceship moved, and now you know it's all pretend.

We'd barely pulled out of the parking lot when Lily pointed to the Circle K on the corner.

"I could see the sign from the yard," she told me. "I'd look at it and salivate, thinking of walls of refrigerated pop and bins of ice cream sandwiches."

Gravel spit behind the tires and stirred up clouds of dust as I turned into the Circle K. Lily asked if she could borrow a ten, and I followed her into the store, watched as she skimmed the shelves of granola bars, bruised bananas, processed fruit smoothies. She stopped at the make-up section and grabbed a stick of mascara, a tube of lip gloss, and green eye shadow, then disappeared into the bathroom.

I waited for her outside in a patch of shade next to a catclaw tree. Barely a quarter mile away, Perryville Prison Complex stood like a row of tombstones against the sun-bleached desert, lassoed by chain link fence and barbed wire. An hour ago, my sister was changing out of an orange jumpsuit, saying goodbye to women she told me went by nicknames. Ca$h, Glitz, Two-teeth. It turned my stomach to imagine my sister among them, identified by a number and the color of her jumpsuit.

The sky was yellow with heat. To the east, monsoon clouds built plum-purple over a jagged mountain range. I'd never felt a heat like this, a heat that steeped under my eyelids and ballooned my lungs. The prison shimmered in and out of focus through the heat waves, and I turned away from it.

Lily emerged from the Circle K looking younger than she had when she entered. Her eyelids green, her eyelashes thick like fur, the dark circles under her eyes hidden beneath cream.

"I got so bored of looking at myself without make-up," she told me, opening the car door and sliding into the passenger's seat. "Men think we wear make-up for them, but it's really to satisfy our own narcissism."

I slid into the car next to her and turned on the air. We pulled back onto the highway, and I was grateful when Lily switched on the radio. Grateful to not have a silence to fill.

Entering the prison, I'd had to remove my belt and my shoes and my earrings. A man in a tan uniform wanded me down and collected my belongings in a small plastic bin: my keys, the anti-nausea pills I'd been swallowing for morning sickness, my Virgin Mary necklace, my loose change, my engagement ring.

When Lily emerged from a back room, she hugged me before I hugged her. She hugged me, and I smelled lemon and cigarette smoke. She wore a pair of jeans I recognized by the hole in the knee, and a crop top that I didn't recognize. Her hair was dyed red, almost the same color as mine, but brighter. A bright, commercial red. It made me think of a time when we were young, pre-puberty, and strangers would mistake us for twins, even though she's older. I'd encourage the mistake by wearing Lily's clothes. In the summer I'd squeeze lemon juice into my hair and bask in the sun until I was almost blonde. As a kid, I was obsessed with the idea of having a double, some-one who shared my DNA, my skeleton, my face. For a month,

I slept on the carpeted floor of Lily's bedroom, thinking that if we slept close enough, our dreams might align.

A guard cleared his throat, and Lily pulled back, ran a hand through her new, red hair.

"I'm done with this place," she said. "Let's get out of here."

I turned to a guard. "Can we?"

He handed me a sheet of paper. "Rules for the parole period." I skimmed. *No contact with inmates or officers affiliated with Perryville.* Lily took the paper from me, crumpled it into her pocket.

"You're good to go," he said, and Lily grinned. Said, "Top shelf, right corner."

She led the way out of the prison. Down the hallway, toward the heat of the desert day, the blinding desert day. She left the prison like she'd been practicing this her whole life.

We found a hotel in south Phoenix an hour out of Perryville. Lily paced the outdoor pool as I booked a room, her eyes squinted against the sun.

Reception told me the only space left was a first-floor room with a single king-sized bed.

"Do you have anything else?" I asked. "Maybe an extra cot? Or a pull-out couch?"

There was nothing. I should have reserved a room ahead of time, but until the moment I pulled into the prison parking lot, I wasn't sure I'd actually come. Until a month ago, I'd had no idea Lily was in prison. I was living in Pennsylvania with my fiancé, hadn't talked to Lily in over a year. I'd assumed she was in Philly, working odd jobs and taking theater classes in the evenings.

I reluctantly handed over my credit card, then joined Lily by the pool. She had her feet in the water, her flip flops stacked by her side. I crouched next to her, and together we watched a palm frond float across the pool's surface. Yellow and green lovebirds chirped in a nearby tree.

Lily saw me looking, and said, "They're not indigenous."

"What?"

"They come from Africa. People used to keep them as pets."

I reached down into the pool. I pulled the water up over my legs, over my knees.

"They weren't good pets. They were too loud, too social. People would release them when they couldn't take it anymore, and so the birds started their own colony here. Far away from home."

She pulled off her shirt, revealing a tan bra, dark around the straps and under the arms where the fabric rubbed against her skin, where her sweat had stained the tan to brown.

"Lily," I said, looking around. A man walking his dog along the pool fence didn't look at us. Lily pulled off her jeans, folded them neatly next to the pool's edge, then dropped herself into the water. She didn't surface right away, but drifted, limbs outstretched, at the bottom of the pool. My skin goosepimpled for her. The air was hot but the water was cold. Underwater, she looked like a sea monster. Her hair haloed her head. The red dye steeped and bled into the water around her, turning it crimson for a moment before fading into blue.

When she resurfaced, she spat water and said, "So, who's the lucky guy?"

I twisted the engagement ring on my finger. She blinked water from her eyes.

"His name's Todd."

Her hair dripped dark constellations on the cement. She reached out for the ring, and I slipped it off my finger and into her hand. She spun it in her palm over the water, slid it onto her pinkie.

"Your hands are smaller than mine," she said. "Prison's fattened me up."

I tried to smile. I tried to look at her like a stranger might. Peach fuzz under her arms. Breasts round and slightly asymmetrical, larger than mine. I looked for tattoos, for drag marks, but couldn't find any.

I'd hoped it would be obvious, the thing that put her in prison. I'd hoped I'd be able to read it on her body. What mistake did she make that she couldn't get out of? I wanted her to tell so I wouldn't have to ask.

Lily handed back the ring and I took it. "So when do I get to meet him?" The band felt damp and unfamiliar from Lily's touch.

"It's up to you," I said. "We're, well, we're pregnant."

Lily pulled herself up onto her elbows, half in the pool and half out.

"A baby. Wow. Congrats. You're not even showing."

I told her it was only eight weeks into the pregnancy, and she laughed.

"It's just, I never expected you to be the one getting a shotgun wedding. Remember when we were in college? You couldn't even swear without blushing. Do Mom and Dad know?"

I felt the skin on the back of my neck burning, so I let

dana diehl   33

down my hair, spread it over the exposed spaces. I could smell myself, the sweat under my arms, the desert dust in my hair.

"Of course they know. They already have a list of names. Dad's started building a crib."

The pool door swung open with a clang. A woman and a little girl with red, wild hair and a shark-shaped floaty entered the pool area.

"Cover up," I told Lily, and tossed her shirt into the water.

My fiancé thought I was in Arizona to help Lily move. When her call came, Todd was working late, and I was busy painting our new condo Cook's Bay blue, a color we'd agreed on. A color that would be our color. I imagined Cook's Bay blue carnations at our wedding, Cook's Bay blue bridal dresses. Cook's Bay baby booties.

The phone rang, and I picked up, paint still wet on my fingers. A recorded message responded before I could say hello: "An inmate from Perryville Prison Complex is attempting to reach you. To accept this call, please press one."

I must have bumped the key, because suddenly Lily's voice was in my ear. "Hi, Danni. Danni, it's me."

She told me she'd been in prison for six months and was being released in four weeks. She needed someone to pick her up.

"It'd be great if you were there for my big exit. I'd ask Mom and Pops, but, well, they think I'm in Belize on a theater scholarship. I just need a chauffeur for a couple of days."

I heard a scream, and it took me a second to realize it had come from my end, not Lily's. I heard the scrape of rollerblades on concrete. Through the window, I watched a band of kids skate by.

"Lily, I can't just."

"It'll be two days tops. You're still in PA? I'll buy you a roundtrip ticket. I'll pay you back."

"Arizona?" I tried to hear past Lily. I tried to hear myself into the room where she was making the call. Was there a guard monitoring the conversation, listening to my hesitation? What time was it in Arizona? Did time go backward or forward as you traveled west? What did it cost her to call me?

"I'll be there," I told her.

When she hung up, I Googled Perryville Prison and found pictures of flat, brown desert and haboobs that turned the sky sepia with sand and transformed the sun into a ghostly disc. I hesitated, fingers poised above the keyboard, then typed Lily's name into the search bar. *Lilian Finn*. I found *Lilian Finn, Scandinavian track star*. And *Lilian Finn, high school salutatorian*. I scrolled until I found her name listed on the Arizona Department of Corrections website. I clicked, and there she was, her mug shot filling my screen. Sideways smile, pulled back hair. I recognized the yellow tank top she wore, an old relic of Myrtle Beach. There was no mention of the crime she'd committed to get there.

I closed the page when I heard Todd's car pulling into the driveway. My heart raced.

How would he react to Lily being in prison? Todd was clean, he was good. All four of his grandparents were still alive. While my family was spotted with mental illness, with cancer hidden in the folds of organs, he came from bodies that didn't betray their owners. I'd told Todd stories about Lily, stories about her wild-drunk college days, stories about her embarrassing me, hurting me. I'd told him the reason we'd stopped talking was that she stole a boy from me. We were too old to steal boys from each other, well into our twenties, but she did it anyway.

I told Todd about it before I knew we'd get pregnant, before I knew he was someone I'd want to be in my life permanently. I told him, "This guy's name doesn't matter. We'd been dating for just a couple of weeks, but I was already really into him. I brought him to our family reunion in Allentown, we had one every year. He hit it off with Lily. I was happy to see her approving of someone in my life. We joked around and drank, they got to talking so I left to hang out with other people. When I tried to find Lily and him again, they were gone." I told him about finding Lily and the boyfriend half an hour later, rolling around in the grass at the edge of the yard, along the tree line where the outside lights didn't reach, where Lily and I used to play Hide and Seek as kids. "It took them minutes to even realize I was there. I'd never felt so on the outside."

Now that we were newly engaged, newly pregnant, I regretted having told Todd this story. A piece of Todd's DNA was entangled with mine now, growing larger and less abstract every day. By revealing this thing about my sister, I felt I had revealed something about myself. A weakness, maybe. Or the potential for weakness. Telling Todd that Lily had gone to prison would make it worse. He'd want to know why I was going to help Lily, and I'd have to admit that it was out of obligation, but also the truer truth, that I wanted to see her weaker than me.

Nausea souring the pit of my stomach, nausea born from joined DNA, I knew I would lie to him. I'd tell him that Lily had apologized, wanted to reconnect, wanted me to visit her in Arizona to help her move.

I'd let him believe she was fixed.

I didn't sleep well with Lily in bed next to me, her weight creating a dip in the mattress, a dip that tried to roll me toward her. I dreamed the baby was a hook in my stomach, unfurling my insides. I dreamed that Lily and I were conjoined at the hip, by a band of skin that snapped us back together when we wandered too far apart.

I woke up early and sat on the edge of the tub, breathing in and out until the churning in my stomach subsided. I could hear strange birds outside the bathroom window. Birds with calls that clawed against the heat. Impostor birds that weren't meant to live in the desert, but found a way.

Around eight, Todd called my cellphone, but I silenced it. I placed it on the sink where I wouldn't be tempted to check for texts.

When I emerged from the bathroom, Lily was holding a Styrofoam plate of food from the lobby. Little tubs of yogurt, jellied toast, coffee in paper cups.

"I should get home," I told her, taking the bread. "I shouldn't be away from home while I'm pregnant. I'm leaving tomorrow."

"I know," Lily said. She sat cross-legged on the bed with her coffee. "I need you to take me somewhere today, and then you can leave. I won't bother you anymore."

"You're not bothering me."

I watched her dig through my suitcase and pull out one of my T-shirts and a pair of cargo shorts. She put them on, and they fit. I realized I'd have to buy new clothes soon, shirts to fit my expanding stomach.

"Can I borrow these?" she asked, and I told her to keep them.

I got ready quickly, anxious to leave the tightness of the hotel room.

I waited as she put on make-up in the bathroom, the same green eye shadow as yesterday. She blended cover-up into her chin and cheeks, over her forehead, spots that seemed unblemished to me. I wondered if she could see something swelling beneath her skin that I couldn't. An infection, a soreness.

"Ready," Lily told me.

Stepping into the car felt like stepping under a magnifying glass, the air too hot to breathe. Lily started to roll down the windows, but I stopped her and turned on the AC.

I asked her where she wanted to go, and instead of a destination, she gave me directions. "Left on Alameda, right on Superstition Freeway."

She directed me onto the highway, and after miles of identical, low-roofed houses, after miles of palm tree malls, I could see that we were leaving the city, entering the mountains.

"Where did you say we're going?"

"Errands."

We pulled off the highway. There were no palm trees here, only Saguaros, barrel-shaped cacti, creosote. I started to get nervous as we saw fewer and fewer cars. The terrain grew rougher, and great red cliffs rose on either side of the road. A brown lizard scuttled across the pavement, and I swerved.

There were things I hadn't told Todd about the night I found Lily with my boyfriend. I didn't tell him the position I found them in. Lily on top, Lily pinning his wrists. Lily letting her hair fall on his face.

I didn't tell him that later in the night, after the boy had left, I found Lily puking in the upstairs bathroom. Lily bent over the toilet, hair damp against her forehead. Lily in a pair of pink Tigger pajamas that I hadn't seen her wear since she was eighteen. And instead of helping her, instead of holding her hair back, I'd murmured, "Slut." And when she didn't respond, I'd said it again, louder. Slut.

I didn't tell Todd that my feelings were more complicated than hurt or angry. I didn't tell him that I called her a slut because that was easier than being jealous. I didn't tell him that when we first started dating, I tried Lily's move on him. We'd been playing, fake-wrestling. I rolled on top, held him by the wrists, he let me do it. It was empowering, liberating, and that scared me. I rolled onto my back, turned away from Todd, while something ugly stirred in my throat.

Lily pointed to a small, shack-like store along the side of the road, surrounded by wooden signs promising "Best Rattlesnake Jerky in Sonora." We'd been driving through the desert for an hour, and this was the first sign of human life we'd seen. I pulled into the lot. Gravel crunched under the car. An old man sat in a lawn chair in the thin shade of a Saguaro, and a fat, white-furred mutt slept at his feet. As I shut off the car, the man shakily stood and disappeared into the shop. The dog stood and licked our ankles as we stepped out of the car.

"Where are we?" I muttered to Lily. It was cooler here than in the city, though I could still feel the sweat collecting in beads under my arms and against the collar of my shirt. I patted the dog on the head, felt the boniness under its fur.

Lily stood so that she blocked the door. "There are people here I need to talk to. It's important, and I need you to just hang back and let me do my thing. It's a gift shop. Look at the stuff, buy something for Todd."

She was close enough for me to see the freckles on her nose. Her skin was rougher than it'd been that night in my parents' house. I could see the build-up of sunburns on her face.

A bell rang as we entered the shop, and for a moment everything was ghostly and dark as my eyes adjusted to the lack of light. The old man stood at the cashier counter. Skinny and pale, a thin brush of hair, cowboy boots.

"Is Chayton in?" Lily asked, and the man nodded to the open storage room behind the counter. Lily stepped forward, and I grabbed her arm.

"I don't know," I said.

She shrugged off my hand. "Try to be cool, Danni," she said, like we were back in high school.

I followed her into the storage room. Boxes of odds and ends towered around us. I read the labels Sharpied onto the sides of boxes: *iron horseshoes, skeleton cactus, shoe strings, gold powder, cowboy bullets, snake skin, bat membrane, javelina tusk.* A single light bulb swung overhead. A wide-shouldered, middle-aged man was taping up boxes in the back of the room. He looked up at Lily. A crimson scar ribboned from his ear to his jaw.

Lily went to him, tip-toed, kissed him on the cheek.

The gesture was too intimate, too gentle, for Lily. The light bulb above her head brought out the red in her hair.

"Danni, this is Chayton," Lily said, turning to me. "Could we have a minute alone?"

Chayton's eyes stayed on my sister with a softness that unnerved me. His hand was on the small of her back, touching her shirt. But no, it was my shirt.

I stepped backward. Lily shut the door behind her.

I found myself alone with the old man, facing the closed door.

"They won't be long," he said to me. He had a voice like wind in a bottle.

I looked at the man's name tag: "Ralph."

"You're pregnant?" he said. He reached under the desk, fumbled through a drawer, and pulled out an unlabeled white envelope. "Take this, and your baby will be immune to snake venom."

I peeled back the envelope's flap and looked inside. Stuck in the bottom crease was what looked like a palmful of ground seeds.

"How'd you know I was pregnant?"

"My wife was pregnant eleven times," he said. "I developed a sense for these things."

I pretended to shop—picking items up off of shelves, rotating them in my hand, then placing them on the shelves again—all the while thinking of Lily and Chayton in the storage room together, the walls close, Lily not afraid of the closeness.

"Everything's a dollar off for you," Ralph said. "Because you met Tim."

"Tim?"

"The store greeter." He waved at the white-furred dog panting in the doorway.

I made an effort to not think about Lily. Todd would expect a souvenir. I could make stopping here worth my time.

But this store didn't seem to have any real souvenirs. Instead, the shelves were piled with dirty horse shoes, polished stones, tiny cacti growing in chipped teacups, boxes of flattened coins. I stopped and looked at a framed newspaper article next to the cash register. It was faded, but I could make out the image of a wreck, headlined: *Thanksgiving Tragedy in Superstition Mountains*.

"The desert is full of ghosts." Ralph snapped his finger and the dog came to his side. "To live here is to accept that."

There was a shout behind the storage door. The dog perked up, and I reached instinctively for the phone in my pocket.

Lily came out, and I caught a quick glimpse of Chayton, his face red, pacing beneath the swinging bulb, before the door swung shut.

"Let's go," Lily told me. She pushed me out the door, back into the parking lot. Dust kicked up around our feet. I heard loud cursing from inside the store, and Lily dragged me into the car. From the passenger seat, she stuck the key in the ignition for me, shifting the car into reverse.

Saguaros streamed by the window, one after another until they blended into one like a flip book.

"What was that?" I asked Lily.

I drove with one hand on my stomach. I'd heard that mothers start to form a connection with their baby while it's still inside them. They'll sing to it, talk to it when they're alone. I'd been surprised to learn this. So far I'd felt nothing but unease.

Lily kept her eyes on the pavement ahead. She said,

"Chayton's daughter was my cellmate my first few months at Perryville."

"Oh. Okay."

"She was only nineteen. She killed herself before I really got to know her."

I glanced over at Lily. She was staring straight ahead through the bug-splattered windshield. My shirt draped over her shoulders, dark with her sweat.

"I knew she was sick," she said.

I didn't ask how the girl did it. I knew that a person could strangle themselves with shoelaces if they had to, or choke themselves with a spoon.

"After she died, Chayton visited the prison. He came to see me."

I wanted to ask, Are you in love with him? Is he in love with you? How would you betray him?

Lily kept talking as I ramped onto the highway and merged into traffic. "I told Chayton today that I have to move on. I'm leaving Arizona."

"Where are you going?"

She put her feet up on the dashboard. "You want to know why I was sent to prison?" I didn't respond. "One of my friends had a boyfriend in for possession. I'd drive her to the penitentiary every weekend so she could smuggle Snickers and love notes in for him. I got to know some of the guys, and started to smuggle stuff in myself. Little keepsakes, mostly. Messages. Mementos. Rings. Pictures of their wives with lipstick stamped in the corner. I was curious about the objects that mattered to people."

"But you were caught."

The desert was giving way to city again. We passed

a billboard for a casino, a mini golf course, a row of identical houses.

I wondered if Lily was telling the truth, or if there was a truer truth she was still hiding. Later, I'd look it up. I'd learn that Lilian was arrested for smuggling contraband into the prison. If she'd been caught smuggling drugs instead of love notes, her sentence could have been years instead of months. She would have spent the rest of her thirties behind bars.

"Don't tell Mom and Dad," Lily said, turning to me. "It'd make our next reunion hell."

Lily fell asleep on the bed, spread-eagle, the Weather Channel muted on the TV. A high of 107 was predicted for tomorrow. Monsoon warning for the late afternoon.

I was feeling antsy and hungry, so I left a note for Lily and ventured outside.

The heat took my breath away, but I expected it this time. I breathed like a lizard. I filled my body with sun. I headed for the lobby, where I knew there was a vending machine. When I stepped through the automatic doors, the sweet coldness enveloped me. The room was empty, a "Be Back in 5" sign placed on the reception desk.

I bought a Big Texas cinnamon roll and ripped through the plastic with my teeth, scanning the front desk for brochures. My eyes fell on a turquoise-beaded necklace sitting next to an empty coffee cup. It coiled over the receptionist's keyboard. The clasp was broken. I thought of Lily preparing to smuggle a love note into prison for the first time. The paper folded under the lining of her sleeve. The rush she must have felt.

The room was empty. I reached for a brochure, then

at the last minute grabbed the necklace, wrapped the chain around my ring finger. I turned. I walked outside, forcing myself to walk, not run. The necklace in my palm felt flat and cool.

I stopped next to the pool and sat on a beach chair. The pool, smooth and bright blue. I waited for the adrenaline, for the sweaty hands, for the elevated heartbeat. I put a hand on my stomach and waited for nausea to set in. I felt nothing. I opened my palm. The necklace curled like a snake between my fingers. It was cheap, I could tell from its lightness and the dark rust stains on the chain. I could see now that the beads weren't even real turquoise.

I jogged back to the lobby, but didn't go inside. I could see through the glass door, the receptionist sipping coffee at her desk, eyes reflecting the computer screen. I placed the necklace on the ground outside the door and ran back to the hotel room.

Lily was still asleep on the bed. I could see a thin line of drool stretching from her mouth. I shook her by the shoulder.

She groaned and slapped away my hand. I crawled onto the bed so that I could look directly down at her.

"When you were with my boyfriend. That was so messed up."

She tried to pull the corner of the blanket up over her face, but I grabbed it and held it back.

Lily groaned. "Danni," she said, "that had nothing to do with you."

"Of course it did. Just tell me why."

"Danni. Danni, I did it because it was fun."

She seemed to fall back to sleep then. Eyes shut, face

relaxed, she looked like a child, and it made me remember a time when we were both young. A time when our parents took us to the swimming hole in north Reading and we took turns diving off boulders, trying to touch the muddy river-bottom before we ran out of breath. The water was cool and vast. Underwater, I felt like an animal, hot-blooded and full of possibility. Underwater, my sister and I would synchronize our movements.

Lily was telling the truth when she said fooling around with my boyfriend wasn't about me. I only wanted it to be about me. What I wanted as a kid I still wanted—to be a double, to have my actions tied to another. But Lily and I had moved past a time when that could be us. I placed a hand on my stomach and felt through my skin for something recognizable. The heel of a foot, an elbow. But it was too early for that.

Sitting on the corner of the bed by the window, I watched distant jets fly through the sky. Jets glinting in the Arizona sun, trailing long lines of white. Tomorrow I would be in one of those planes, arching across the map, back to Pennsylvania where soon I'd be married, where soon I'd have a baby that shared not all of my DNA, but half. I bend my body in half so that my lips were only a few inches from my belly-button. I begin to sing.

It's been two days since we were swallowed by the loneliest whale in the world. Two days since we caught in its trachea, and having nowhere else to go, crawled into its damp cave of a belly.

We are brothers. Our first night in the whale, we took turns sleeping, resting our heads against the other's knees— something we hadn't done since boyhood afternoons on our father's shipping vessel. We used our headlamps to shine halos against the whale's ribcage. We cast shadow puppets against the vertebrae. We located and then avoided the large intestines.

The whale's song vibrates through our bones, tickles our ear canals. When one of us speaks, we have to say, *Speak up. I can't hear you. Speak up.* We try to read each other's lips and find we can't.

You might say we'd been asking for it. We heard about this whale on the news—a whale with a fifty-two hertz song, too high-pitched to be understood by its brothers and sisters—and were seized by a desire to see it. We took to the sea in the masted ship we'd inherited from our father. For seventy-two days, we tracked the whale from Anchorage to Panama. But in the end, the whale found us. Off the coast of Central America, it was as though a hole had opened in the sea. The indigo waters spilled over themselves, seagulls screamed. Our ship tilted, and we slid between the beaked lips. We clung to what we thought were our last minutes of life. We have no children or wives, so we tried to picture the face of our mother and the face of our beloved beagle, Blaze. We tried to picture the faces of the last women we kissed, but the images we conjured were only composites, hybrids of every woman we'd ever loved or lusted over or tacked above our bunk in glossy brilliance.

We waited for our worlds to go dark.

Before long, we're eating krill. They're clear-bellied, feather-limbed. They feel like onion skins in our mouths, and we have to eat handfuls to feel like we've eaten anything at all.

We wish our whale would swallow something more substantial. Ruby-fleshed tuna or tiny octopi with suckers like jelly rings. After a meal of krill, the thought of manta ray makes us salivate.

We've just gotten used to the whale's eerie song, the persistent tremor in our chests, when it goes quiet. Except for the gentlest rise and fall of its stomach, the whale is still. We hear the slow beat of its heart, the crack of stored oxygen in its lungs.

Asleep, we agree, and we crawl on our hands and knees to the space where the belly becomes throat. Soft flesh narrowing to a ribbed tunnel. Here, the whale's heartbeat consumes us. We count eight beats in sixty seconds. We wonder if the whale knows if we're here, if she sensed the moment she became a container for something smaller than herself. In sleep, can she dream herself inside her own ribcage? Can she dream us brothers, us men, casting shadows and lighting her up in the dark?

Thinking these thoughts, we feel our *we* dissolve into *I:*

I'm afraid I'll die here, and my skeleton will traverse the seas forever in the stomach of a beast.

I can still remember the briny scent of our father's shoes when he returned from a sea journey.

We turn onto our backs, we slide back into the cradle of the belly. We hook arms as we fall.

In the belly of the whale, we invent similes to pass the time.

Sitting in a whale is like sitting in a tuba's spit valve.

Sitting in a whale is like sitting in a bowl of leftover ABC soup.

We cast shadow puppets on her ribcage, and we give our shadow puppets stories. The swan swallows the fox swallows the dog swallows the spider. Our shadow puppets' mouths move but make no sounds. They lost their voices after so much chewing.

We trade quotes from the old black and white submarine movies our father would watch after dinner when we were children. On land, submarine men were tall and sharp-suited, but in the depths of the ocean, they wore frayed, high-necked sweaters. They wore boots with puddles in the heels. In the tight, underwater corridors, they brushed shoulders, and they held each other without shame.

We figure a whale is a kind of submarine. We sit back to back. We imagine what it means to be a whale, not contained but afloat. Miles of ocean below, unknowable sky above. Enclosed in the whale's loneliness, we feel like brothers again. We called each other brother, but it's the first time in years that it's been true.

The whale sings again. As she sings, her body shivers. She seems to be shaking herself awake. Her voice moves through us like we're nothing, and it feels impossible that her kin will never understand this song.

We don't know when we'll be able to speak again, so we raise our voices with the whale. We yell without words. We try to match our pitch to her hertz, we try to find her pitch in our guts. We were never singers. We used our voices only for shouting commands to our crewmates, for ordering second and third and fourth pints, for saying *I love you* to our mother and then to women we wanted wooed. Now, our voices say, *We hear your loneliness. We have it too.*

The whale tilts into a dive. We tie our shoelaces together so if one of us falls into intestines, we both will.

The bag worms were the first thing to go wrong. It was July. Late morning. The girl and boy woke to webby nests ghosting the branches of their apple trees.

The boy and girl were new to commitment, only seven days married. They still marveled at the mountain-valley shapes their bodies made beneath the sheets. They were still growing accustomed to each other's smells—she thought he smelled like upturned earth, he thought she smelled like freshly cooked pasta. They stood shoulder-to-shoulder at the window, peering out through the screen.

"Where do they come from?" the boy wanted to know.

"How do we get rid of them?" the girl asked.

Up close, they saw that the nests swarmed with small caterpillars. Black, the size of poppy seeds. Cradled in the heart of their nests, the caterpillars looked like they were swimming through a fog. The boy thought of astronauts untethered but unafraid. The girl thought of stubble on the boy's chin, hairs scattered and wiry, sharp enough to leave the skin around her mouth raw after they kissed.

She took a branch off the ground and imagined wrapping the webs like cotton candy and feeding them to the burn barrel. But the boy placed a hand on her arm and pulled the branch free of her fist.

"Let's leave it," he said. "It's not hurting anyone."

dana diehl   51

He leaned the branch against the tree, like it was a problem solved.

The months before their wedding had been all excitement and newness. The girl's friends took her to a pole dancing class in the city where she discovered the secret strength of her thighs. The boy's friends took him quail hunting in Appalachia. The girl went for her first bikini wax. The boy started doing tricep dips on the dining room table during dinner dates.

Together their lives were objects accelerating without friction. Their parents gifted them Pyrex, dish towels, comforter sets. Words that, side by side, sounded like items in a recipe. The boy and girl found a small ranch miles away from their apartment homes, a house on a hill that overlooked a creek and a scattering of homes and miles of Amish farmland, and purchased it using money they'd saved in their mid-twenties for a price the realtor said was unusually low. The reception was held in a fire hall strung with white Christmas lights. The boy and girl danced the foxtrot, the electric slide, the conga, the Macarena. A firefighter drove them around the block in the engine and let the girl flip the siren when they went through an intersection. In tux and dress, the boy and girl looked like famous people, they looked unlike themselves. They posed for photos, they smeared icing on each other's cheeks.

They left the city for their new home still in their wedding clothes. They drove through the dark, learning their new town through the silhouettes the trees made against the sky.

"I would do anything for you," the boy said in the girl's ear as they pulled into their new driveway.

"I'd do anything for you, too," is what she said.

For the first time in weeks, the girl's phone wasn't ringing, wasn't filling up with messages from the florist, the caterer, the photographer, the bridesmaids. She turned the phone off, unnerved by its silence.

That night they consummated their marriage loudly. The girl felt disconnected, and the more disconnected she felt, the louder it seemed she had to be. She felt the boy's shoulder blades, the animal fur of his thighs. She felt the gritty sweetness of icing residue on his cheeks. She felt the hill under their home, she felt the Amish family at the bottom of their hill, knuckles thick as roots—even the girls', from pulling stubborn carrots from soil every summer. Tucked under covers, she felt the creek and the quiet mud-creatures asleep under its current.

This is mine, she thought to herself. This is mine.

The day after the bag worm nests appeared in their apple trees, the girl started noticing them everywhere: in the neighbors' vegetable gardens, on the underside of mailboxes, spilling out from the inside of birdhouses. Each nest containing a fist of black baby worms. She tried to look beyond them, to the haystacked hills, to the fields plowed by wide-shouldered horses. She couldn't explain to her husband why each time she looked at the nests, she felt a dark, slimy thing turn her gut.

"It's because you don't understand them," the boy said.

They had decided to spend their three-week honeymoon at home, their new home—to save money, to spend time together instead of next to strangers on planes. The past eight days had blurred into one. They slept late, bumped shoulders in the hallway, mixed up their toothbrushes in the bathroom drawer, figuring out what marriage felt like.

The boy went to the living room and dug through the still-packed boxes until he found a wildlife encyclopedia. He returned to the girl and flipped it open in her lap. He pointed to a photograph of a black worm, yellow striping its back like a spine, body covered in small hairs like morning stubble.

He read that they weren't really worms, but caterpillars, and after they were caterpillars they'd become moths. Their Latin name: *Malacosoma.* He read out loud. He read that their nests were called tents, and that their tents were made of layers of silk that formed tiny rooms, and that in the early mornings the caterpillars would gather in balls to keep the cold at bay. They might live their entire caterpillar lives in their tents with their brothers and sisters. Then, when it was time for them to become moths, they'd crawl out of their tents, across branches, down tree trunks, to the forest floor to spin their solitary cocoons.

The average tent caterpillar completed its life cycle in a little over two months. The caterpillars were driven by something in their DNA they couldn't control. Their actions decided by the angle of the sun, the temperature of the ground, the twist of a gene. The whole of a female moth's life—mating, laying eggs—might take place in fewer than twenty-four hours.

The girl thought, If our marriage is successful, we'll still be together fifty years from now. How do you fill fifty years? It scared her, this thought. She felt the slope of her life plateau. Getting married had been so easy, everything moving toward it, marriage the next obvious step, no one asking what happened in the after.

Later that day, the boy suggested they walk down the hill, so they slid on their walking shoes, they locked the windows and the back door. They held each other's hands, sweat gathering between their palms. They passed between houses with swings in the front lawns, plastic deer statues in the gardens, snagged screens and silver satellite dishes. Collies chained to trees, a cardboard sign for "fresh eggs." They reached the creek, deep and swift-moving. A bridge crossed the water, and a half dozen kids sat on the guard rail in bare feet, in swim suits and cut-off shorts and wet T-shirts stuck to ribs. The boy and girl stood by the creek and watched as the kids took turns jumping, cutting through the humid air, and disappearing into the water below. They emerged screaming with cold and adrenaline. Wild things.

The boy smiled at the kids, waved, and the girl pulled on his elbow to turn back. As they climbed the hill back to their home, the boy pointed to a splinter of movement on the road ahead. The girl saw that it was a bag worm, full grown, like the one in the book, inching along the curb, probably looking for a place to spin its cocoon. They found dozens more, scattered across the black pavement. The girl accidentally stepped on one, spread it across the sole of her shoe. She wiped it against the curb. Inside, the worm was green. She hadn't even felt its body break.

The boy pulled into the driveway with a canoe tied to the roof of the car. "Happy honeymoon," he said. The canoe looked used, its bottom a maze of scratches and nicks. He told her he bought it from a guy in the next town over. The canoe had been sitting in the man's front lawn with a For Sale sign taped to its side. He lifted it off the roof of the car and held it in his arms like an oversized baby. The girl slid her palm along the canoe's underbelly and pulled back with spider webs tangled around her fingers.

"Want to give it a try?" the boy asked.

For two hours the girl had been alone in the house. The boy had left for groceries, and for the first time in days she found herself alone. She took a shower just to feel the heat rolling off the water, refused to worry about the water bill. She allowed herself to think thoughts she'd feel guilty thinking around the boy. How yesterday had been her ex-boyfriend's birthday, the boyfriend who played hockey, whom she'd liked for shallow reasons: his hockey gear like plates of battle armor, his slap shot quick and deliberate. How once an older man had asked her to move to Thailand with him and she'd turned him down, how sometimes she'd check the weather in Bangkok and think, In another life I'm wearing a sundress and sipping Chang beer poolside. She was dizzied, thinking of how many paths she'd failed to follow to their ends.

The girl wiped the spider webs from the canoe onto the thighs of her jeans. "Let's go," she said.

They drove down the hill to the creek, parked next to the bridge. The boy held the canoe steady in the water as the girl stepped in. She felt it sink under her weight, the water moving to fit the canoe's shape. The boy pushed it into deeper water and leapt in. The girl had never paddled a canoe before, so he taught her how to move just the skin of the water, how to steer into the current instead of against it.

They paddled to the bridge. The kids, who always seemed to be there, bare feet dangling, hooted down as they passed underneath. The boy looked up, hooted back. When he saw the kids with their dirty callused soles, he saw his future.

He saw Christmas trees hung with tinsel, scabbed knees that fit in the palms of his hands, warm pancake mornings.

"Should we turn back now?" she asked. She was afraid the kids would start jumping, disrupting the surface of the water.

The boy shook his head. "Paddle on."

The creek led them away from the road, away from the houses. Birch trees, oaks, aspens, Sassafras trees leaned over the water. A heron flapped on a stony riverbank. Gnats clouded above half-submerged logs, fish moved like phantoms under the canoe. The girl could see a line of white at the next bend, rapids frosting the surface of the creek.

"We've got this, don't worry," the boy told her.

He wanted to feel the river muscle them. He wanted to feel it spit in their faces. The canoe rocked and steadied as they entered the rapids. The canoe scraped against a rock, invisible under the foam. The girl looked back at the boy, who grinned in response. The canoe broke free from the rocky creek bottom and shot forward. The girl's hands ached, but she realized she loved the speed. They were flying. A slick boulder reared out of the rapids, and they steered around it, only to scrape against another, smaller rock. Before they could fight it, the canoe had tipped, and they were dumped.

The girl never went completely under. She clung to the rock that tipped their canoe, fingers vice-like, feeling her shorts and bra and shoes balloon with water. When the current finally pulled her loose, she flipped onto her back, kicked off her shoes. She let the creek pull her, tug her. She paddled toward the bank, arms pebbling with goosebumps. She pulled herself up onto the reedy shore, gasped for breath.

Only then did she remember the boy. She looked out

over the creek, its loud, white surface. The canoe, belly-up, bobbed downriver. No boy. No top-of-head. No hands-grasping-for-air. She was no longer a girl with a boy. She was a girl starting over. She was a girl back on top, the slope of her life tilting before her. Free to go to Thailand, to sell the ranch on the hill. So easily she could climb, dripping, out of the rapids that pulled him under.

Downriver, the water was still. It was there that the boy emerged, thrashing and shirtless, kicking off his waterlogged shoes. The girl watched him breast-stroke to the shore, watched him collapse on the opposite riverbank. Lying in the mud, he was hardly recognizable as her husband. He could be a drowned muskrat, or coyote, or baby deer.

She ran barefoot down her own bank until she reached shallow water. She waded across the creek, which now only went up to her ankles. She approached the boy as he was coughing water onto a dry stone.

"I'm sorry," she said. "I'm sorry."

She was still imagining him gone. She was frightened by how easy it was.

The boy coughed up creek water. His spine ridged. He coughed until he laughed.

"So maybe that wasn't the best honeymoon present," he said.

The canoe was gone. The girl imagined it following the river to its mouth, slipping into the Atlantic. She imagined it finally filling with water and sinking. Sliding along the Mariana Trench, crabs nibbling at its frame, eels nosing at its scraped-up bottom.

The boy and girl, barefoot, half-dressed, walked back home.

. . .

That night in bed they embraced in the dark, their hair still wet. The girl realized that she didn't notice the boy's smell anymore, couldn't smell him when she tried.

Through the part in their blinds, the girl could see the bag worms' nests like small moons stuck in the branches.

She said to the boy, "Why did you want to marry me?"

He didn't ask why she wanted to know. He told her that when they'd first started dating they went hiking at Bald Eagle Mountain, hoping to find a red fox that was rumored to be living in the forest. Almost immediately they found it, drinking from a pool, nose wet and paws muddy. It felt to him like a fairy tale, when the heroes go into the woods and find what they're looking for without even trying. He told her that he liked having her with him over the holidays, playing chords on his parents' piano and teaching his baby cousins how to play Mary Had a Little Lamb.

As he spoke, she thought of the creek frothing with foam, so much colder than she would have expected. If she had been the one to be dragged under, he would have saved her. She knew this. She thought of him underwater, tumbled by the creek. Even then, he must have been reaching for her. While she was saving herself, he was trying to save her. This made the girl unexpectedly angry. Angry at herself, or angry at him and his lack of doubt.

"Where do you see us in the next twenty years?" she asked.

She felt him shrug. "Well," he said. "Here. Happy. Doing what makes us happy."

The girl sat up in bed. She told the boy she was going to get a snack. She didn't turn the lights on as she moved through the hall, finding her way with a hand against the wall, trying to see the house in a way she never had before.

In the kitchen she rummaged through the junk drawer. Her fingers found the box of kitchen matches. She took them through the front door and onto the stoop. She stood barefoot, letting her eyes adjust to the night. There was a full moon and she could see the slither of the creek below the hill and the sharp points of roofs.

She approached the apple trees. Up close, she could see that they were almost empty. Only a few caterpillars left. The rest had crawled to the ground, looking for hollow logs or curled leaves in which to weave their cotton-candy-soft nests. By the end of August, the yard would be full of moths. The last month of summer would crisp the grass. It would shrink the creek, revealing its rocky bottom, exposing sandals lost by the bridge children, crawdad skeletons, a rusty paddle wedged between stones. Moths would mate mid-air and lay pearly eggs in the crook of trees.

She didn't want their future. Every season following the same predetermined patterns, their power of choice taken away.

The boy had told her to leave the nests alone, and maybe next year she would, but this year she couldn't.

She took a match out of the box. Struck it. Listened for the whoosh of heat.

She wanted the boy to kneel in their bed and part the curtains to watch her. She wanted to act and not know how he would react.

The first match went out so she lit another and cupped it in her palm. She lifted it to the lowest nest, held it there until the small flame became a big flame. She blew it, gently, to life. One by one she lit the caterpillars' nests until the apple trees were alight with isolated balls of fire. She stood back and watched, relieved by the sight of the nests curling into nothing.

She heard the boy at the door. "What are you doing?" he asked.

The flames clung to the branches like hungry, orange birds. The girl joined the boy in the doorway. She breathed, smelled smoke. They waited.

My daughter comes out of the bathtub crying.

She says she's found a spot, a dark shiny spot on the skin below her bellybutton. She lifts her shirt to show me, and I recognize the curved back of a tick, soft as an eggshell, shaped like a teardrop. I run my thumb over its hard-shell back, and my daughter squirms.

It's the first time I've seen my daughter's bare stomach in six months. She's seven, and since around Christmas she hasn't let me see her naked. A year ago, I was still bathing her every night. A year ago, she'd tie a towel around her waist like a loin cloth in the morning and leap from couch to couch in her bare, pink, new-animal skin. Now, she changes with her bedroom door clicked shut. Now, she pulls the shower curtain around her body like a cape when I enter the bathroom to retrieve toilet paper rolls. The other moms at her school tell me this is normal, that girls become self-conscious about their bodies earlier than boys, but still its unsettling to have a body that was once part of my body hidden from me.

My daughter crawls up onto the counter, lies on her back, and lets me roll her shirt up below her ribcage. I find a flashlight in the junk drawer and tell her to hold it steady so that the light is on the spot. I don't say the word tick yet.

I retrieve tweezers from my bathroom. I place a hand on her belly to steady my wrist, and she sucks in. She says, Cold hands. I pull back, warm my fingers in my armpits, try again. The tick barely looks like a tick. It's the size of a pencil tip, buried deep enough into her skin to look like it's part of her. A mole, or a birthmark. I pinch it close to its head, avoiding the tick's engorged belly. I pull. My daughter's skin is soft under my palm. She smells like rising bread.

The moment I lift the tweezers, she eels out from under me onto the kitchen floor, sprints into the living room to turn on the TV. I drop the tick onto the white back of a receipt, and tape it in place with Scotch. It doesn't move. I hold it to the light. I can see all eight of its legs. I can see its belly swollen with my daughter's blood. In this moment, it is more her than I am.

My daughter goes to bed at nine, and I take my laptop to the front porch. I can see the shapes of deer moving through the neighbor's front lawn. Probably the same deer that brought the tick to my yard, to my daughter's stomach. I light a cigarette, and the deer raise their heads in unison. Half-chewed grass hangs from their fleshy lower lips.

I log in to my OkCupid account. I have three new messages, from men who write that I have a nice face, that they love a woman with kids, that I look like someone they'd like to take out for coffee. All three men are at least ten years older than me. They have haircuts that remind me of my daughter's father. I erase their messages.

A year ago, I couldn't date. A year ago, I'd go to work with jam-stains on my blouses, come home to my daughter screaming, laughing, reaching always wanting. Now, my days contain unexpected pockets of free time. The photos on my OkCupid account are ones that I took myself. Alone in the afternoon, I carry my camera in my purse. I set the self-timer

animal skin

and balance the camera on a ledge, on a root, on the roof of my car. I have ten seconds to arrange myself. I know exactly how long it takes to walk from one end of the frame to the other. I know how to cock my hips so that my shirt rises just an inch above my pants, so it looks like an accident. I know how to move so that my cesarean scar is hidden under the flap of my T-shirt.

A tick will reach you where you are most vulnerable. Armpits, soft paunches of belly, the crook of your neck. It's attracted to your warmth, to the small vibrations your body makes without knowing it. A tick will stick itself to your skin with its own saliva, bury itself in its blood feast. If left alone, a tick will swell to a light-gray blue.

My daughter snores in her bedroom. The sound travels through the open windows, and I wonder what she was dreaming about. Once, my daughter was a fist of cells, connected to me by a thread. Once, my blood was her blood. I felt her knuckle against my skin and knew where to find her. I think of the tick, only half full, still alive under clear tape, and in that moment I want to let it go. I want to follow it through my house. I want to let it be my guide. My guide back to the soft, hidden places that I've forgotten how to reach.

Justine watches South Carolina disappear with the sun through the smudged airplane window. She's fifteen, body like a blade of grass. Three weeks ago, over Christmas break, her father called to tell her mother he wouldn't return from his five-month study in Anchorage, that he was staying to track the migration of humpback whales with his co-writer, Kara. Justine listened from the phone in the laundry room, hand cupping the receiver, holding the sound in place.

"Their song is changing, Laurel," he said, and her mother hung up. Went to her room and locked the door and didn't emerge until an hour later, her eyes red. That night, Justine doodled whale flukes up her wrist as her mother bought two one-way tickets to Scotland over the phone.

"It'll be an adventure. Winter in Scotland. We'll eat deep-fried Mars bars and climb mountains and look for Nessie," her mother said, speaking with her hands. "We'll stay with my friend, Calum. He's studying the separation of the continents from Pangaea. Exciting, right?" She wore new lipstick, the shade of fig-flesh, and had her hair tied back for the first time in years, the lines of her face pulled to hard angles. It made her ears, her forehead, look too exposed, a landscape stripped of trees.

"How long will we stay?" Justine wanted to know.

"As long as we want."

In the weeks before the flight, she ordered Justine a

British nature guide and asked her to memorize the flora and fauna of northern Scotland. Over dinner, she had her recite the four endangered flowers, the six popular nesting sites for seabirds, and the most poisonous spiders and where to find them: "The tube web spider, found in the toes of shoes. The huntsman spider, in banana crates, on pieces of fruit."

Justine didn't really believe her mother would go through with the trip. She'd always talked about going, about taking a break from her office job with the Department of Natural Resources, and never had. But then, after Christmas break, she called Justine's school to let them know Justine wouldn't be returning for the spring semester. A day later, she came home from work with a box that held her cactus, the lopsided mug Justine sculpted when she was six, a geode she bought in New Mexico. She pulled suitcases from the attic and wiped silkworm cocoons out of the corners with the back of her hand. Before saying goodnight, she told Justine stories of puffins nesting in rocks, of mountains as soft as flannel, of castles built on sleeping volcanoes. Calum lived on an island called Skye off the northwestern coast. Except Justine shouldn't call it an island anymore, she should call it an isle. And a lake was no longer a lake, but a loch.

Justine's mother lived in Scotland for a year during college, studying geology at the University of Glasgow. Sometimes, when Justine was younger, her mother would pull out the slides, yellowed and dusty, and project them onto the blank white cinderblocks in the basement. Images of herself—younger, thinner, with glasses like owl eyes. Poised on top of a mountain. Cradling quartz and sandstone in the crook of her arm. Doing handstands on a beach, her belly—now a mystery, hidden behind baggy shirts—exposed and flat and

68   closer

pale. When Justine was younger, she danced across the projections and cast shadows into her mother's memories, sliding so that her mother's face would cover hers.

Now, they travel to Scotland together. "You should sleep," her mother says, leaning back into her jacket, which she's folded into the shape of a pillow. Her shoulders touch Justine's between the narrow seats, rubbing bones under skin, and Justine leans away. She presses her forehead against the glass and feels the vibrations of the plane move through her skull.

Within moments, her mother is lulled to sleep, and Justine is wide awake. She watches the progress of the plane on the digital map built into the seat. Watches as the plane travels out of North America and soars over the Mid-Atlantic Ridge, arching under Iceland. There are four miles of air between her and the water. Ten miles between her and the seafloor. Miles filled with fish, with whales, with eels and squid. She's supposed to feel like she's being taken somewhere, but instead she only feels like she's being taken away. Justine counts the time zones as they pass and thinks about her father in Alaska. "Soak it all in," he said to her on the phone that morning. "Be good. Make the most of every second. I'm sorry I can't be there with you." She imagines him eating deer meat in his kitchen, graphs of whale songs strewn across the table, coyotes stalking in the shadows behind the shed and pipes freezing and cracking in the walls. She imagines him looking into the darkness, waiting for the earth's axis to change.

Scotland is browns and greens and gray skies, cold fog suspended in the air, cutting hills and trees in half at the end of the runway. When they get off the plane in Edinburgh, Justine's mother breathes in. Her eyes close and the soft spots of her face tighten. Justine mimics her, feeling her lungs fill with dampness. A seagull cries overhead.

Calum waits for them outside the terminal. Justine recognizes him from the Scotland slides—a body always blurred in the photos, in motion. While her mother has visibly aged, a crown of gray where the dye's faded, he looks much the same. Garnet-colored hair. Skin leathery like a bat's wing. Body thick and boxy, built for being close to the earth. As they approach him, her mother adjusts her shirt, pulls her hair back.

"Pleased to meet you," Calum says, shaking Justine's hand. His accent is like gravel, and his hand cups hers like an oyster shell around a pearl.

Justine knows Calum from his handwriting, messy letters that spike and run together. Handwriting that indicates both seriousness and curiosity. As long as she can remember, her mother has received packages from him in the mail, every six months or so, with a rock bubble-wrapped inside, a scribbled note on loose-leaf paper. Limestone from the southern coast of Britain. A piece of sea glass with a flower-burst patter. Red sandstone from Dundee. He never labeled them. "It's a challenge," her mother explained, examining the fissures with a magnifying glass at the kitchen table. While Justine's mother pored over the gifts, her father, long and skinny like Justine, would disappear into his office and play recordings of whale songs, their high-pitched calls bubbling and sinking through the house. Justine loved the songs, their unpredictability.

Calum's car is small and smells of rock dust. Justine sits in the back seat with the suitcases and listens as her mother points, exclaims. She waves to a crag rising above the steeples and points of Edinburgh. Arthur's Seat, she calls it. Formed by a 350-million-year-old volcano. And later, Argyll Forest, where Calum taught her to kayak. Rising dark, almost purple, from the distance. Covered in trees that are leafless, but draped in light green moss like spider webs.

"How did you end up back on the Isle?" Justine's mother asks as they leave the forest.

"After my divorce," Calum says. "She moved to France. I moved back to the Isle when they found those dino-saur prints and fossil-hunting took off. Got a proper job doing digs and working in the Staffin museum. Laurel, you look just like you did twenty years ago."

Justine flips through her nature guide and scans hills outside the car window, watching for magpies, for red squir-rels, for puffins lost inland. But the car travels too fast for her to focus, and soon it's dark.

After traveling north for hours, they cross a long, arch-ing bridge onto the Isle of Skye. Calum turns down a street that follows the coast and stops at a one-story house with dark windows, white stucco walls, and a front yard paved with tiny shells instead of grass. It's cold and windy outside the car, so they rush inside. Justine stands in the middle of the living room with the suitcases, not knowing what she can touch, as her mom flits from wall to wall and picks up framed photo-graphs of landscapes, flipping over magazines held down by quartz and bookends shaped like eagles. She hovers next to a map of Pangaea over the fireplace, Africa sandwiched against South America. North America pressed against Europe. The room smells like spices and smoke. Calum switches on lamps, casting shadows. He turns on the television, and a weather report lights up on the screen. Justine looks at the Doppler radar map of Scotland, with its irregular coast, its inlets and rivers like veins. She looks at the way the weather swirls, appears and disappears, so different from South Carolina, where weather moved in big, green, predictable masses.

"Justine, you'll sleep here." Calum leads her to the end of the living room, where he's hung two quilts off the ceiling beams, sectioning the room in half. He pushes them aside to reveal an air mattress with blankets folded at the end, a curtained window, and a lamp sitting on the floor. "Sorry it isn't more. Usually it's just me here."

Justine nods, pushes past him. Sits on the mattress.

"I know it can be overwhelming," he goes on, still holding the quilt back. "I traveled to America once, when I was young."

Justine nods. She wants quiet now. She wants to close her eyes and be in a familiar place.

"Goodnight, Justine," her mother says as Calum drops the curtains. Justine doesn't answer. She crawls under the blankets and pulls off her jeans and sweater, kicking them to the end of the mattress. She thinks about finding Calum's phone and calling her father. Imagines closing the gap with the punch of numbers, the transportation of invisible particles in the air. She falls asleep to the sound of the house moving, the wind whistling through the empty spaces.

In the morning, Justine sits in silence with Calum as her mother, wrapped in a shoulder-to-ankle robe, rushes from behind a closed door to the bathroom. Justine picks at a piece of toast smothered in strawberry jam, and twenty minutes later her mother emerges in clouds of steam, her hair black in its wetness, her cheeks rosy. She looks like a stranger here.

"I want to see the Isle," she tells Calum. "I never made it up here while I was in college. I've heard about the glacial troughs and aretes."

"The arêtes?" Calum corrects.

Justine's mother blushes. "You might have read the essay I wrote on Arbroath. On the sedentary rock erosion? Back in college, I was one of the first people to take record of it. I was thinking I'd follow you around, maybe try writing again."

They turn to Justine.

"How would you like that? Want to take a tour of the Isle?" Calum asks, but Justine shakes her head. She doesn't want to get back in the car, trapped in metal, doesn't want her mother to quiz her on the fauna of the island, or to hear about the geology of the land. She itches to move. So, as they drive off, Justine watches them go from the front lawn.

Calum's house is on its own at the end of the road, but she can see more homes and a church steeple, a mile or two in the distance where the coast curves toward the mainland. To her right, there's a sharp incline of brown grass, no trees. Across the street, a gray strip of beach, the water covered in a thinning mist. She walks to it, her shoes bending to the rocks, slipping on the yellow growth. She reaches the water, and the sea laps up to her feet. There are broken, purple sea urchins in the tide pools and clam shells with white flower-patterns growing on their backs.

This is the ocean. The Atlantic Ocean in Scotland. Justine thought it would be different, wider, from this side. Like when, six months ago, her father saw the Bering Sea for the first time and decided it was worth leaving home for. When he recognized something larger than his own life.

Justine tries to remember the things her father taught her:

The Atlantic is two thousand miles wide. Six miles deep.

If the ocean froze over, it would take over a year to walk across.

The oceans move in a clockwise motion, exchanging water, sharing it.

A whale might see every continent in its lifetime.

Justine can still see the mainland, green and hazy, in the distance. She decides to walk along the coast, walk until the mainland disappears and it's just ocean, nothing but water between her and America. Maybe then she would feel her new place on the planet.

As the rocky beach turns to cliff a few yards up from the waterline, Justine climbs along it, walking through grass that's wet and swampy with dips and hollows disguised by piles of heather. Her feet and ankles sink through, and the cold water is a shock. It fills her sneakers, leaves her gasping for air. She takes another step and sinks in mud to her thighs. She gasps and looks back, searching for the plated roof of Calum's house. It's out of sight. All around her, as far as she can see, are brown, barren hills and gray water ending in haze. No seagulls. No porpoises or whales breaking the surface, blowing water. For a terrifying moment, she believes she's the only living organism on the earth. Is this all Scotland is? Is this the Scotland her mother longed for?

Justine turns back, pulling her feet up out of the mud. She follows the coast, struggling through the heather, slipping over the bouldered coast until it takes her to Calum's house. She undresses in the foyer and runs, naked, to the bathroom, where she wraps herself in towels, where she washes the mud off her jeans in the sink. Brown water puddles between her fingers and spins down the drain. After pulling on sweatpants, she hides the damp clothes under the mattress in her corner of the living room. She doesn't want her mother to see.

Justine's parents had been fighting for months when her father left for Alaska. They always argued in the bedroom, door closed, but the sound traveled through the cracks. Her father spent too much time at work. Her mother was distant, disinterested. When Justine's father took the position in Anchorage, her mother refused to see him off at the airport. Justine had to watch him pass through security and disappear into the terminal alone. She watched planes take off from the window, unsure of which one was his. She tried to remember which way was west.

He sent her letters while he was gone. Letters that described the aurora borealis spread across the sky, icicles growing into elaborate shapes overnight, and how to extract clear water from bark using a Swiss Army knife. Letters with waxy, fireweed leaves pressed between the pages. And bark rubbings of Alaska Cedars. Trees that, he told her, Northwest Coast Indians would carve into canoes. Wood durable enough to take to sea. He sent her pictures taken underwater, of schools of fish in a twister formation. Of a woman in scuba gear, posing, suspended, next to a beluga whale, a dark braid sticking from the back of her head like a tail. *Kara*, the picture was captioned. He explained that she had grown up in Southern Belgium, was only thirty-three, but had already traveled to twenty-two countries and helped discover a deep-sea fish that lit up like a rainbow when mating. The envelopes were never addressed to her mother, so Justine hid them. The last envelope, the first one since he decided to stay in Alaska, simply contained a CD, whale songs scrawled in pen across its case. Justine had slipped it into her backpack, unopened.

Calum and her mother return from their drive late in the afternoon, an hour before the sun sets unseen behind the gray clouds. Her mother has pockets full of shale and chalky quartzite that she places on the mantelpiece. "You missed out," she says. That night, in Calum's kitchen, the two pull out old photographs from her mother's semester abroad and lay them across the table, and when that's covered, across the hardwood floor. Forming a breadcrumb trail. Forming a story. Justine hovers in the corners of the room and watches over their shoulders. She recognizes places from her mother's slides. The mountain. The beach. The monument. But these photos are taken from different angles, with different focuses. They extend the pictures where her mother's slides cut off. Her mother took pictures of landscapes, the people blurred, but Calum favored details. A jellyfish caught among the rocks like a drop of water. Foam circling a pint of beer. The two of them, arms around shoulders, freckly and holding rock picks. A tight shot of her mother's face, smiling, eyes looking at something past the camera lens, dark red mud smeared across her right cheekbone. When they leave the room, Justine kneels on the floor and combs through the photos, looking for familiar blemishes on her mother's face, following the trail of fingerprint smudges around their edges.

For the next two days, a hard rain pelts the house. It drums on the windows, drowns the flowerbeds at the end of the driveway. Calum leaves for work before Justine wakes up, and she and her mother spend the day inside, scouring the bookshelves, working their way through Calum's tea collection. Justine finds a book on sea life and learns that sound moves differently underwater, five times faster than on land. She learns that a whale song can travel for three miles in the ocean. Calum returns in the evening with mud-stained pants and hair slicked down by rain. On the second day, he comes home with news. He has convinced his boss to give Justine's mother a part-time, temp job assisting him with field work.

"Thank you," she says. She squeezes his arm and volunteers to make dinner. Justine notices that her mother's voice is different when Calum is home. Her accent shifts. About to aboot. Thank you to thenk you.

The next day, her mother goes to work with Calum. She wants Justine up and out of the house, exploring on her own, so Calum asks an Isle boy named Thomas to show her around Kyleakin, the nearest town on the island. Thomas meets Justine at the post office. He's seventeen, tall and long-limbed, with dark hair cropped short enough for her to see the shape of his skull. He has an accent that's guttural, difficult to understand. Justine hopes he'll be able to take her to the Pier Coffee House, or maybe to the mainland, where she can buy a new pair of sneakers or boots. Instead, they pass the time walking the docks. After lunch, Thomas takes her to a pub, small and smelling of fish and beer. He pays with pound coins, and the bartender slides her short glasses filled with liquid that's amber in the light, that burns her throat and the back of her nose as it goes down. She throws up over a wall into a patch of whitlow grass on her walk home.

After that, she explores alone. Her mother and Calum leave to do field work in the morning, and she walks into

Kyleakin. She walks from one end of town to the other, counting the houses. She buys fish and chips from a restaurant and nods to fishermen who come into dock at nine with nets full of squirming, silvery fish. In the post office, she thinks about calling her father, but realizes that a five minute call would cost all the pound coins her mother has given her. A week passes in this way. She examines palm trees on street corners. Palm trees whose seeds, Calum explained, traveled from the Gulf Coast to Scotland in the North Atlantic current. She walks in the rain, cocooned in rain gear, and lies on the top of crags, waiting for the weather to change, wondering what Calum would think if he saw her, eyelashes wet and brown, Scottish mud seeping into pours of her skin. Maybe she would pass as her mother, decades younger, still a girl.

On the other side of the island, her mother buys her an old Nikon camera. Justine already has a digital camera, but her mother says they aren't the same. Digital cameras are all about efficiency, while with a film camera you have to take your time, get to know your subject. The next morning, Justine feels brave and uses her change to take a bus up the coast. She gets off when the barren land, spotted with sheep, turns to forests. She's packed her camera, an egg sandwich, and her nature guide. It feels good to be among trees again, walking through clovers, through carpets of pine needles. In the forest, distances are contained rather than open and never-ending like the ocean. She walks until the trees are thick and close together, and then she climbs. Bark against palm. Soft space behind the knee hooked around branch. Using muscles that she hasn't exercised in weeks. Her fingers slip on the weblike moss, but she likes the challenge. Justine climbs and climbs until the branches are thin and young and won't support her weight, and then the sun breaks through the clouds for the first time, and she leans her face against the trunk. Warming it. Feeling for the movement of sap underneath. Willing the movement of water up, up through its pores.

They have been in Scotland for two weeks. Now Justine's mother and Calum both return in the evening with muddy pants, rock dust on their shirts. Justine's mother wears her hair up, and over dinner they talk about the new fossils shipped to the Staffin museum, the quartz uncovered on the southern shore. Her face looks shiny and young. Justine hears that lilt in her voice and wonders if already her mother's palate is changing, adjusting to Scotland. Justine goes to bed early at night, not because she's tired, but because she doesn't know what to say around Calum and her mother, who talk about nothing but their adventures in college, about work and stone and plates shifting and grinding, slowly.

"The separation of Pangaea is what defines our continents," Calum murmurs as he flips through topographical maps and rubbings of fossils.

Justine hears her mother reply softly, "I don't think we're going to make it."

"Why?" asks Calum. He's lit a fire, tossed on pine logs that fill the house with a smell like earth and syrup. It catches in Justine's throat as she breathes. She's in her bed, but awake, watching the light of the fire cast shadows against the quilt.

"We haven't held hands in two years," her mother says, "We can't sleep in the same bed, can't sleep when we feel each other there. It's like living with a stranger. He has some theory about the whales' songs changing, but I really don't think he's right. He's always following theories, always working. And I can't care anymore. It's like all my care has dried up."

Behind the quilt, Justine turns in her bed, pulls the covers up over her head. The smoke coats the inside of her throat and her lungs, and she wishes that the wind would blow stronger, working its way between the boards and pulling the house apart. She presses the blanket to her ears, and their voices fade. She hears laughter. Calum hums.

The next day, Justine leaves the coast, follows a one-lane road behind town, where sheep chew on grass next to the pavement. As she passes them, they bleat and scatter on black hooves. She uses the last of her film taking a photo of a four-wheeler driven by a bearded farmer, a sheep dog leaning against his back. The dog is tense, hair slicked, tongue red and flapping. Dust rises in plumes around the wheels, and the farmer nods. Speaks in Gaelic: "*Mattiva.*" Good morning. Then, he's gone and everything is quiet again. Quiet but not quiet. The wind doesn't stop.

She walks until the road arcs back to the ocean. Fifty yards away, the coast slopes up into cliff, and she walks toward it. Approaches it hesitantly. It's maybe two hundred feet high, casting a dark gray shadow across the waves. Burnt-yellow grass covers this side of its face, and she grabs handfuls of it, using the strength of its roots to crawl-climb up. Her fingers close around empty snail shells, around an otter rib embedded in the soil. Pieces the ocean spit back onto land.

The grass turns to stone, and she tests it with the palm of her hand, feeling for weak points. But the stone, gray, flecked with white, its grain running parallel to the sea, feels solid.

She moves upward, placing her weight on her feet, feeling through the soles of her sneakers for the easy holds. Then, she looks down. She sees the water spreading out beneath her, pushing a line of foam, crashing against the lower cliff. A black-backed gull dives below her. The knuckles on her left hand shake, slip. She feels sick and retreats.

Justine walks to the coast every day after that, searching for sea glass or smooth stones in the shallows until she summons the courage to try the cliff again. Each time she promises herself she'll go farther. To the leafless shrub on the outcrop. To the brown markings that look like a face. But whenever she sees the sea spinning beneath her and imagines the fall, imagines sharp rocks hidden by sea foam and jellyfish lurking in the protected tide pools, she turns back.

One day, three weeks after she and her mother moved to Scotland, walking through the sheep fields to the coast, she hears an engine. She turns and sees Calum, alone in his car, on the main road. He pulls over, and Justine walks to the window.

"Where's my mom?" Justine asks.

"She's back at the museum, cataloging samples we found on the west coast. I thought I'd give her some space and pick up lunch at the house."

Justine rubs her toe against the blacktop. Calum asks her if she needs a ride.

"It's fine. I'm just walking to the coast."

"Oh, that's okay. I'll take you."

Justine climbs in, and Calum shifts into first gear. As he drives, Justine adjusts the passenger seat. She pulls it forward, lowers the headrest. Her mother's dried boot prints are on the mat, the smell of her peach body wash in the fabric of the seat. When they reach the dirt path that leads to the cliff,

Justine points and Calum pulls over. She quickly readjusts the seat, and they get out. Calum follows her to the narrow, gray strip of beach, and Justine wonders if now he'll leave her, but he matches her pace as she makes her way to the cliff.

"Do you walk to the coast often?" Calum asks.

"I like to come here and climb."

She sees Calum eye her knuckles, her palms. They've grown rough, callused over the past few weeks.

When she reaches the cliffs, he says, "Show me." She hesitates, then scrambles up the bank. When she hears his footsteps behind her, she continues. The path is familiar to her, and she's confident. She uses her entire body to climb, swinging her hips, hooking her knees around holds. She stops where she usually does, muscles burning, eight yards beyond where the grass ends. As she clings to the slope, Calum scrambles up beside her.

"You've got good rhythm," he says as he jams his fingers into a crevice she hadn't noticed before. She sees a small, half-moon scar between his first and second knuckles.

Justine leans her cheek against the rock. It's cold, damp, and she has the sudden, odd desire to lick it. She imagines it tasting bitter, of salt. She imagines rolling that taste around on her tongue like a marble.

"Let's climb higher," Calum says.

He takes the lead this time. Justine tries to follow, watching the way he uses his surroundings. A fist around a branch. A heel lodged in a crack. Holds that she'd never find on her own.

"How'd you learn how to climb?" Justine asks through breaths.

Calum slows down, waits for her to catch up. The

rock face is smoother here, and Justine fears a slippery patch or a dead end. She's forced to catch her breath by Calum's elbow, her knee brushing the heel of his foot. "I grew up on the Isle," he says down to her. "Thirty years ago, there wasn't a bridge to the mainland. My brothers and I were hard pressed for entertainment. We'd race and swing from holds like we saw gulls do and flap at each other with our arms, trying to push each other off. We liked to climb in the rain, in the wind, to feel nature fighting."

Justine looks down at the water with its invisible currents, its invisible monsters, and gulps.

"Did you teach my mom to rock climb?" she asks.

"No."

Justine breathes. Her hands cramp, and she wants to move again, but every obvious hold seems too far out of reach.

"Close your eyes," Calum tells her. "You're using your eyes too much. You have to get to know the rock to climb it. Feel its face."

Justine lowers her eyelids, unclenches her right hand. Lets it slide up, against the rock, feeling for the fissures. When she finds nothing, she opens her eyes. Her breath comes quickly. She climbs back to the ground, not waiting to see if Calum will follow.

A month since Justine and her mother arrived in Scotland, Justine starts to worry that they will never go home. She worries about missing school, wonders if they'll let her rejoin her class after missing so many weeks. That weekend, it snows for the first time since they arrived. Wet flakes that melt in the yard but coat the stones by the coast and catch in the sea foam.

Justine walks into town to buy hot chocolate, and when she returns to Calum's house, he's already there. The shoulders of his sweater are dark with melted snow. His hair is wet and clings around his ears.

"Your mother," he says, out of breath. "She's had an accident, might be a broken rib. I've already taken her to the doctor, but I think you should be there. She was going in for X-rays when I left."

Justine grabs her backpack from the living room and they rush out into the snow, into the car. The wheels spin on the gravel driveway. The seat back is reclined all the way and smeared with mud, and Justine pulls it forward as they leave Kyleakin, brushing off the dirt with the back of her hand, leaving it there once she realizes she has nothing to clean it with. She feels in her bag and asks Calum if she can put a CD into the player. It's her father's recording of whale songs. Songs that could travel miles and miles through empty oceans. Nothing to bounce off of but silent, suspended fish. She had almost forgotten about the disc, here in Scotland without a CD player.

"Dad plays their songs at home all the time. It calms me," she says, and Calum nods as she opens the case and slips the CD into the slot. She recognizes belugas in the first track, wonders if they're from Alaska.

The only doctor's office is on the opposite side of the island, in Kirk. They make it through three whale songs before they reach it. Calum leads Justine inside the small, thatched building, points her to the door. When she knocks, her mother replies, "Calum?" from inside.

Justine opens the door. She barely recognizes the woman sitting on the examination table, wrapped in a thin hospital robe. In the bright, sterile light, it's like her mother has shifted to a higher resolution. The robe is open in the back, and Justine's eyes follow the curve of her spine. The skin is almost purple where bone presses against flesh.

"What happened?" Justine asks.

"Nothing, I'm fine. We were examining the west shore for trilobite fossils, and I slipped on a wet patch. It's probably nothing serious."

The doctor enters the room.

"Ma'am," he says. "We didn't find any cracks. Only a bruise. Painful, but an injury that will heal on its own."

"Thank you," says her mother. And then to Justine, "See? Not that bad."

"I'll just need to do a final check before I let you go," the doctor says.

He pushes aside the robe, and Justine's mother's belly and upper leg are exposed. Justine is surprised to see blue veins like tributaries of a river inching up her thighs. She's surprised to see a pouch of flesh under her mother's rib cage. The veiny parts that hang from her upper arms. Justine looks at her mother, and for a moment, their eyes meet. Her mother doesn't blink, and Justine turns away. She looks at the wall.

"Really, Doctor. It's fine," her mother says. "Barely hurts anymore."

The doctor removes his hand, and her mother pulls at the fabric, covering the parts of her body he revealed. She changes back into her clothes quickly, silently, with a curtain separating herself from Justine.

Calum jumps to his feet as they enter the waiting room.

"Thank God it was just a bruise," he says. "I'd feel terrible if you were seriously hurt on the job."

Justine's mother nods and places a hand over her ribs. When they reach the car, she reaches for Justine's wrist.

"Are you okay?" Justine asks.

"I'm fine. Let's walk to the water before we go home."

"Sure, mom."

They make their way slowly down the road to the coast, Calum a few steps behind. Justine knows they're close to the water when the wind picks up, wild, cold. Her mother curls her spine protectively as snow sweeps off the roof of a house and then straightens again. A block farther, and they're at the sea. For the first time, Justine looks out at the uninterrupted Atlantic. Gray. Misty. Stiller than she expected.

When they've reached the water, Justine's mother kneels and pushes away the snow. She pulls out a handful of egg-shaped stones.

"Sandstone. Carried down through Europe on a glacier in the ice age."

Justine kneels next to her, sees her mother wince as she struggles to remain balanced on the balls of her feet. A gull dives and scoops a fish from the water a few yards off shore. Justine reaches a hand out, instinctively, and catches her mother's shoulder.

Her mother pulls another rock from the snow, this one thin and gray, and breaks it in half. She points to a spiral-shaped fossil where the stone cracked.

"A brachiopod," she says. "Extremely common here. The only other place where they're found so frequently is the coast of New England, where the countries used to touch."

Justine ladles snow into her hands and presses it between her palms, packing it together, watching it melt out from between her fingers. Her mother drops the stone, and

Justine follows the path of her gaze out over the ocean, out toward the horizon.

"Hello, America," Justine says.

Her mother waves.

That evening, Justine tells her mother she's going on a walk. All afternoon, her mother has wandered through the house, stacking her notebooks and graphs into piles, stopping on the arm of the couch every few minutes to place a hand on her ribs.

Justine thinks about walking to Kyleakin, watching the sun set against the bridge connecting it to the mainland. Instead, her feet carry her down the familiar road to the cliff. The snow stops as she walks. Already, it's melting to slush on the streets, the ground too warm to keep it in place. In the fields, sheep break it apart with their hooves. When Justine sees the gray line of water on the horizon, she thinks about how close, how crowded, the ocean felt when she first arrived. Now it's just empty. Like space in between instead of space itself.

Justine reaches the cliff, and she climbs. Without hesitation. Hand over hand. Using her elbows, her toes, the tips of her fingers. Her palms pass over a fossil of a shell, over a piece of quartz embedded in the cliff. On an outcrop, she finds a broken eggshell the size of a hail stone, cool blue and speckled. Where the cliff pleats in on itself, she wedges herself in the hollow, pressing her knees and elbows against the walls, suspending her body in place.

All around, the wind howls. In cracks. In holes. In hidden caverns. The muscles in Justine's wrists feel strong, hard, and she closes her eyes. She presses her cheek against the mountain and imagines that she can feel it moving. Imagines continental drift in reverse, the countries puzzle-piecing themselves back together. Magpies and crows fly in the same sky. Whales share a single, massive ocean, no landmasses to stop their song. And rock collides with rock, buckling under the pressure, deciding to fold.

My boyfriend believes in the healing powers of stones.

I'm a pharmacist at the CVS on University. I spend my days sorting pills, counting pills. I find comfort in their hidden potential, their weightlessness, their clean, edgeless shapes, and the way they pebble at the bottom of a prescription bottle. I believe in magic beans produced in factories, by chemists and cool-metal machines. I don't believe in energies, in mystic forces that can't be measured.

My boyfriend and I have been dating for two months. We met in the hospital, where he was dropping off a friend, and I was visiting my father. I brought him home with me—to my small house I bought myself, with hardwood floors, a built-in saltwater fish tank, and a hummingbird feeder that I always keep full with sugar water—and found that I never wanted him to leave. Now, I come home to quartz nestled in the heels of my sandals, emeralds tucked into the pillowcases, agate in the aquarium, and sodalite on the windowsills.

When I find the stones, I place them in a bowl by the front door. My boyfriend gets sneakier with his hiding places. One morning I find a sapphire mixed in with the coffee grounds. The kitchen sink clogs, and when I twist apart the pipes, I find a small onyx pearled in the slip-joint elbow.

One evening, I spread the stones between us on the comforter. "They have to go," I say. The stones, each a different color, each unnaturally smooth, create small craters in the fabric. "They're breaking my house."

"You're too tense," my boyfriend tells me. "You need to learn how to accept help. Charoite would help with that." But still he scoops them into his duffel bag. I hear the thunk of their stone-bodies settling on the floor, and I'm happy. In the morning, I return to the pharmacy and spend the morning sorting blue, green, white, pink pills into containers. In the afternoon, I help customers. I listen to their lists of complaints, the aches that come from their bones, from their lungs, from the space behind their eyes. I hand them paper bags of pills.

After work, I drive to the hospital. I walk down whitely-lit halls, comforted by the cleanness, by the predictable shapes. I pass the bench where my boyfriend and I first met.

When I enter my father's room, machines beep in a slow rhythm. He hovers in half-sleep, his arms connected to tubes connected to pouches of liquid. His skin is yellow, his hair is cropped short. Barely even my father anymore. I pull back the blankets to adjust his robes, and I find that his body is covered in splotches of color. For half a second I think they might be flowers, or butterflies. But no, they are stones. Amethyst between his fingers, ruby in the hollow of his throat, rose quartz tucked under his knees. Stones to align the chakras, attract serenity, and sharpen dreams. The stones glimmer along his arms, dip like hummingbirds into the cavities of his armpits. He's become half rock, half man.

I want two things at once. To gather the stones into my arms, to drop them one by one out the window, watch them shatter in the parking lot below, crack against car windows, reveal their broken insides. To stuff them down my father's throat, to see if the magic would work then.

But I don't do either of these things. Instead, I watch

the movement of my father's chest, the rise and fall of flesh and stone. I take the smallest stone, the size of a pea, lift it from my father's shoulder and hold it to my own lips, its smooth surface still warm. I touch it with the tip of my tongue, wait for the moment when it'll start to dissolve.

My father made snakes fall in love. Cobras
and rattlers, mambas and boas, Chihuahua Mountain
Kings and Mexican Hognoses. Snakes that would normally
never meet, or if they did they'd eat each other, tail first. Me
and my dad lived south of Kitt's Peak, in a corner of the desert
too hot for mirages. Our house was surrounded on all sides
by saguaros and pits with concrete walls where my dad bred
his snakes. Every other day, he'd remove them from their pits
with cloth nets to try new pairings, new matches. The snakes
he bred were more beautiful than their parents, more
dangerous than their parents, uglier than their parents. They
were button-backed, were diamond-eyed, were ridge-
nosed. Each one was the first of its kind, and he let me hold
them in my palms like other kids held monsoon toads or butterflies.

He told me, "Baby snakes are the most dangerous, because they don't know to conserve their poison." He told me,
"But they're also the most gentle." He told me, "The chance
of this snake being this snake is one in an octillion."

When the cobra-rattlers and mamba-boas and
king-hognoses molted their first skins, he strung the
skins around my head like crowns. He draped them over
my neck, tying neck to tail in an infinite cycle. I loved
the snakeskins because they were ghosts of themselves. The
snakeskins had smooth, pea-smooth eye sockets and

ribbed bellies. They made a rustling sounds like dry grass when you breathed into their mouths.

There are many endings to this story.

In one version, the cobra-rattler's mother, the rattler, escapes and bites me on the thigh underneath the tire swing. She bites, and I feel the poison ink under my muscles. When my dad finds me, he rolls up my jean shorts and puts his lips to the bite. He sucks at my leg. Sucks hard. I feel his teeth sink into my skin like buttercream. My father sucks the poison out of my leg, and he sucks out some of my blood, too. I see it on his chin, and it makes me laugh. We are both fine.

And in another version, my father sells all his snakes to other breeders, who will make even more beautiful snakes, more dangerous snakes, more ugly snakes in different snake pits, in different states, in different deserts.

And in another version, my father swallows the poison meant for me and goes blind. Now, in the spring, I collect the snakes' shrugged-off skins. I drape them over the blades of my father's ceiling fan so on hot days he can hear them whirl and rustle. I take the snakes into his bed, and pinch them under the jaws while he pets their scales. Which snake is this? I'll ask. *Grand Canyon Whipsnake, Shovel-nosed Ratsnake.* He gets it right every time.

And in another version, I ask him, "Why did Mom leave?" I ask him, "What if Mom had stayed?" And because I'm still a child, he doesn't have to give me an answer. Instead, he tells me, You have her ears. You have her gummy smile. When I'm thirteen he dates a woman named Zalma. He stops telling me what I have of my mother's, and instead tells me what I don't.

And in another version, I grow old. I grow to be sixteen. I am sixteen and can't believe how many more years I have left to be alive. I am sixteen, and finally allowed to date. My father sets me up with a boy who. Imagine if you guys had kids. I begin to suspect that I am just another one of his snakes.

And in another version, the snakes stop breeding. The boas strangle the rattlers, the kings poison the hog noses. My father's new snakes become orphans, and then we learn that they are sterile. Still, year after year they shed their skins. They make ghost after ghost for me to drape around my neck, hang from my hair. They mate with other orphan snakes. They lay eggs that are hollow, never knowing that the cycle ends with them.

to date a time traveler

He time travels in his sleep. You learn this the morning after your first date at the dive bar that never checks IDs. You'd drunk so many whiskey sours you had to spend the night on his futon, and as you're sneaking out of his dorm in the early morning, embarrassed, ready to never see him again, he sits up in bed shouting *Alamo! Alamo!* in a gritty, Spanish accent, different from the low, soft voice you'd heard the night before.

The longer he sleeps, the farther back he goes.

Stage 1: He sees his mother smoking Cigarillos at Woodstock.

Stage 2: He's with Shackleton on Elephant Island, tasting smoked penguin meat. The sound of seal songs travels up through the ice.

Stage 3: Swash-buckling pirates, women weaving tapestries as their husbands fight wars on distant islands, glacial summers.

The REM cycle is when things really pick up. Over coffee, your second date, he tells you he's made it back to the Cretaceous period, where he saw a triceratops take down a T-rex—*cool, right?* On your third date, a picnic by the river, he says he once saw Jesus feeding mallards in Bethlehem. Sometimes he experiences the past from the outside, an invisible pair of eyes. Sometimes he slips inside the mind of a spectator, feels the pooling of sweat on his collar bones, the movement of air through the nose as if it's his own air, his sweat. You soon realize that normal dating rules do not apply. You remember something your mother told you when you were sixteen: *Only trust a man as far as you can throw him.* But you've never met a time traveler before, and you're intrigued. He has dimples just like your grandfather did, and he wears blazers with elbow patches, and this makes you trust him. One night in his dorm room, over Styrofoam containers of Pad Thai, he asks if you want to go steady and you say Yes. His dimples show and he can't look you in the eye and you melt for that kind of vulnerability.

Your time traveling boyfriend sleeps in on weekends and takes you on drives in the afternoons. Windows down, corn stalks whipping, he describes the smell of the Edinburgh castle in spring of the Iron Age. He explains how to load a musket. When you ask about his own history, though, he changes the subject. You begin to think of him as a deep blue glacier. You read once that glaciers contain small pockets of ancient air, trapped at the time of the glacier's formation. But the glaciers are melting now. They are releasing all of that old air into the atmosphere. Mixing, slowly, old with new.

After the drives, you take your boyfriend to parties hosted by the frat boys in your Spanish class. Your boyfriend is shy about his time traveling, but after you've had a couple of drinks, you can't keep quiet. *He's so talented,* you insist to the DJ. *He's practically met Kant,* you tell the mini-skirted girls in line for the bathroom.

Your time-traveling boyfriend doesn't seem happy at these parties. He gravitates to the corners of rooms: to the fish tank in the kitchen filled with Yuengling bottle caps, to the Godzilla statue made out of beer cans and sticky with Coors

Light residue. When you find him, he kisses you quietly, even though your mouth is slick with beer and lip balm.

Let's go to sleep, he says.

Your friends motion to you from the dance floor, shimmy under blue lights, skin flawless and icy. You feel your time-traveler boyfriend's hand, warm as a seashell, cup your knuckles. You leave the dancers, follow him out the door.

He dreams of snow, of Wooly Mammoths, he dreams he's crossing the Bering land bridge. You stay awake, watching his eyes move under their lids, wishing you could see what he sees.

In December you call your mother to tell her you have a boyfriend. *Okay*, she says. She says, *Maybe you shouldn't come home for Christmas this year. Your Dad and I are going through a rough patch. You might be happier at school.*

Condensation inches up the windows, and you draw circles on the glass with your pinky.

Your time-traveling boyfriend helps you with your American History final.

Your time-traveling boyfriend takes you to see *Braveheart* in the theater and talks over the action—*Wallace was wayyy taller than that.*

You stay on campus over winter break, and your boyfriend goes home to New Jersey, four hours south of your university. You wander the empty hallways of your dorm, checking for unlocked doors. When it snows, you close your curtains to the cold. Your boyfriend calls you every night before bed. Sometimes you hear a young girl's voice in the background. Sometimes you hear a man yelling, and you can't tell if it's with anger or enthusiasm. Sometimes your boyfriend falls asleep with you still on the other line and you wait for someone, his mother maybe, to silently hang up for him.

Your boyfriend tells you, *I wish I could travel farther. How far?* I ask him. *What do you want to see?*

And he answers, *The beginning. I wish I could see the beginning.*

He always seems on the edge of an explanation, on the edge of finding the right way to order the words for you.

When your boyfriend returns to campus, you're waiting outside his room. He pulls you inside and tells you he's met a woman who can help him.

In my dreams, he says. *I've met someone in my sleep.*

You think, Queen Elizabeth? You think, Cleopatra? You know he's seen her once before. Only her ankle, actually, as she glided on a palanquin through Actium, but still, Cleopatra.

But no, he tells you, it's no one famous. It's a pirate girl who sailed on Calico Jack's ship. He tells you she wears fish hooks for earrings. She's an orphan. He's seen her twice.

She's the first person I've ever seen more than once, he tells you. *I remember wanting to see her again, and I did. If only I can hold onto my feelings for her, maybe I can use them to propel myself back farther. Maybe I can control my dreams.*

He still loves you, he reassures. His dream life is separate from his awake life.

You don't leave your boyfriend, because how can you be jealous of someone long dead, someone who probably died at sea, someone whose bones turned to dust, to fish food? In the weeks that follow, he tells you about other women he

to date a time traveler

meets, women who he is sure hold the key to his dreams. A cave maiden who slayed a Mammoth with her bare hands. A wild horse tamer and a leather tanner. You spoon him in his too-small twin bed, wondering which one he's with tonight, how they are helping him in ways you cannot. You feel for his dimples as he sleeps. You remind yourself you can't be jealous of a ghost.

Tell yourself ghosts are not competition. Let your boyfriend sleep in on Saturdays and buy him chocolate donuts in exchange for pterodactyl anecdotes. Let him run with Aztec warriors at night, and let him take you on picnics to Gettysburg during the day. He'll make you scones inspired by King Arthur's Court and chicken wings that aren't quite as tasty as saber-tooth tiger, he says, but close.

One afternoon, your friends, friends you haven't talked to in weeks, ambush you after class. They say they miss you. They say they saw your boyfriend asleep on the lab table during Chemistry. Even the professor, dropping books on the table and shaking the back of his chair, couldn't wake your boyfriend up. You shrug, say your boyfriend has been under a lot of stress, walk off.

But really, you're afraid. You've noticed your boyfriend swallowing Melatonin and Tylenol PM before bed. You don't sleep in your own room anymore, afraid to leave him alone, afraid that without you anchoring him to the now, he'll succumb forever to his dreams. You try asking him about present-day things. You ask him about his family, about his sister, about his father. But he shakes these questions off.

I can't think about them, he tells you. *They'll only distract me.*

What do you think you'll find? you ask him. *If you*

ever make it to the beginning?

He thinks. You're imagining the long-deceased women he's met in his dreams and feel more than a flicker of jealousy.

Then he says, *I don't know. That's the thing. Maybe the Big Bang. God.*

You don't ask how long he'd have to sleep to get back that far. Instead, you try to be supportive. Say, *I time traveled once.* Say, *I flew out of London on a Friday and landed in Newark on Thursday.*

You wake him up only once. He's twitching in his sleep. He moans in a way you can't identify as pleasure or pain, and this scares you. You grab him by the shoulders. He's shirtless, his skin unfamiliar and sticky with sweat. You feel his blood beating under his skin. He won't wake up at first, and you throw back the sheets, blow hard into his ear, pull at the skin on his elbows until he gasps awake. Looking at you, he scrambles out of bed and falls against his desk, scattering papers, knocking over the pocket watch you bought him for Christmas. He's shouting in a language you don't recognize. *Ukryć dzieci, kochanie. Oni nas znaleźć. Zaraz, gdzie ja jestem?*

It reminds you of your first night together, when he woke up speaking in Spanish. In a few moments he'll be back to normal, back to himself. *Calm down,* you tell him. *It's okay.*

You try to hold your boyfriend by his shoulders, but he brushes you away.

Nigdy nie będzie moją rodzinę, he says, eyes wide and panicked.

You reach for him again, and this time he pushes you hard. You slam against the wall, your elbow knocks into the

to date a time traveler

television, which falls to the tile floor. The screen cracks, sparks.

Keep it down, someone shouts from a neighboring room.

You sit in shocked silence. Your back tingles with pain. Your boyfriend stands with his fists raised, his eyes narrowed with suspicion. For the first time, you realize you fear him, have maybe feared him all along. He taps the broken television with his bare toe.

We've got to stay quiet, you tell him. *We've got to stay calm.*

Your boyfriend glances at you, then walks to the door. He fumbles with the door knob for a moment before he's able to pull it open.

No, you say. You follow him down the fluorescent-lit hallway, down the stairwell, and out onto the dark campus. You're both in pajamas and bare feet, and when he slips onto the lawn and the thin skin of snow, you follow him.

Your boyfriend kneels in the snowy grass, and you stand behind him. You can feel the cold aching into your feet and up your ankles. You know your boyfriend must feel it too, but it seems to quiet him. You watch his back as his breathing slows and his shoulders relax.

When he stands up, he's himself again. You can see it in the familiar droop of his shoulders and the way his hooks his thumb self-consciously under the elastic band of his pajama pants.

You take a step toward him, but he holds up a hand. *Wait*, he says.

Why? you ask, and he shakes his head.

I almost made it, he said. I was so close. *I was alone*

in a dark forest. I could feel myself shrinking. I was devolving. But then, then you pulled me out of it.

He sighs. He walks past you, back toward the dorm, leaving ghostly footprints in the snow.

You think you'll follow him, but then you don't. Instead you just watch him get smaller and smaller until he's reached the building and disappeared inside the dark doorway. You are still barefoot, but you don't feel the cold like you did a moment ago. The streetlights glow over foggy streets. The snow is melting. You realize you'll return to your own dorm tonight. You wonder how far you can walk before the sun comes up.

The woman with forty-three children is dying. A spot in her left lung, the size of a balled baby fist. Too late to remove.

The woman with forty-three children is sixty-five. She lives in a neighborhood a train ride outside of Philly. When the news comes that she is dying, twenty-four of her children are home in her fifteen-bedroom house, eleven are in college in upstate New York or Amish country Pennsylvania or New Jersey, one is in Morocco on a Fulbright, two are chasing casting calls in Hollywood, one is a freelance collage artist living on a friend's couch, three are working office jobs in the city, and one is out of cellphone range on the Appalachian trail. But when they learn about the spot, the spot on the lung, they stop what they are doing and fly or drive or walk or hitchhike home.

The woman with forty-three children barely fits on the daybed her sons and daughters prepare for her in the living room. Children require largeness, and the body shifts itself to acquiesce. Bones thicken like hard candy. An emptiness grows in the stomach, grows larger with each child until it refuses to heal.

Many years ago, the woman with forty-three children was a child herself. Her mother was a midwife. She watched woman after woman spread her legs, revealing insides pink like bubblegum. They opened like origami cranes, revealing babies with velvet skin. On the outside these women were red, sweaty, white-knuckled, faces wrinkled and pinched. On the outside, they were wide feet, wide hips, skin striped with lines that reminded her of silver trails left by slugs. But inside, each contained a secret world, a secret softness, a secret sweetness.

There were never fathers.

Or there were fathers, but she didn't see them. It was easy to father, and so she didn't think of them. The fathers were on the exterior, pacing in hallways, clutching toilet bowls, fetching ice. Always elsewhere.

The woman with forty-three children lies on her day-bed, a spot in her lung, and looks up at her children's faces. She never thought she would die. She thought she could cheat death by multiplying, by spreading her DNA over the earth. By making herself large. Not just pregnant-large, but planet-large. She wanted to have more sons, more daughters, more than any other mother before her. Between 1725 and 1765, a woman named Vassilyev gave birth twenty-seven times to sixty-nine children. Between 1943 and 1981, Leontina Albina had fifty-five children, lost eleven to an earthquake. Between 1910 and 1941, a Pennsylvanian miner's wife gave birth to fifty children and still brought tins of water to the mines every afternoon. The woman with forty-three children fell short.

Dying on the daybed, she's surrounded by herself. Her children cradle her chin with their hands, they lean their faces against her thighs, her belly, her soft upper-arms, and it's her cheeks she feels against her skin.

The woman with forty-three children feels the cavities in her body like a deep ache, the cavities she could never keep full enough. She thinks, a mother's body is a house full of rooms that are always being left.

the mother

In this dream there's a fisherman on a dock, wrestling at the end of a taut wire. As Nalin stops to watch, leaning her head against her husband's shoulder, the fisherman pulls out a boy, hook-in-mouth and thrashing. The boy has seaweed in his hair and shoots a stream of water from between his lips. His clothes stick, muddy and wrinkling, to his ribcage, and as the fisherman pulls him out of the water, he screams. It's time to go, her husband says, pushing the small of her back. Nalin wakes. She hears rain drumming on the roof, against the chimney, in the cracks between the walls. She sits up, feeling her bones crack, and breathes. She wonders, briefly, if she's floated out to sea.

In the morning, there's a dark, yellowing patch on the ceiling above their bed that makes it look like the house wet itself. The river out back is swollen. It pushes against its banks, touching the bases of the hemlock trees that line the yard. It makes Nalin, still in her night shirt, want to walk to the river's edge and touch it, dipping her hands into the current, feeling around in the reeds for what makes it move.

      Through the bathroom window, she can see neighborhood boys dressed like pirates floating down the river on a fleet of inflatable mattresses. Eye patches and crooked mustaches Sharpied onto their faces. Red bandanas. Cardboard swords, limp from rain, brandished at each other. There are orange swimmies strapped to their upper arms, looking so out of place. "Argggh!" they shout as the current catches them, spirals them. Nalin's husband joins her at the window, wrapped in the smell of coffee, hair thin and misplaced. Calvin. Cal. Cal, the miner. Cal, the tunneler, making a living directing coal and copper excavations. Nalin's friends made jokes when they first started dating, now almost thirty-five years ago, when they were still in college. About him "digging her."

"So much rain," he says, watching out the window. "It's got to end soon."

"Of course," Nalin says. But she can imagine the forecast. The big, green mass moving across the map on the television. This is one of those rains that will fall and fall and never stop.

Nalin leans her forehead against the glass. One of the boys' rafts is sinking, and he doesn't fight it. The river gulps his thighs, his hips, his waist. "Man overboard!" the others shout. "Mind the sharks!" Their drawn-on eye patches run, streaking down their cheeks and coloring the creases in their skin. The boy laughs, water up to his neck. Nalin wishes she could be there with him, wishes she could take him by the wrist, affirming the movement of blood under his skin, and pull him to shore. Cal reaches an arm around her and rests his hand on her ribcage. Nalin breathes until the window fogs around her face, masking everything but the top of the trees.

By early afternoon, the rain is carving a pond in the dip of the backyard. A dark spot identical to the one in the bedroom has formed in the walk-in closet. The water drips little pools into Nalin's high heels, smears and blurs the colors of Cal's ties,

the mother

gets into a box of shoulder-padded work suits Nalin hasn't worn in decades. She pulls the clothes, all of them, out of the closet and lays them across the floor. A wedding dress. A tux. A homemade sweater knit with red yarn.

Nalin's mother calls, the only person who still uses their landline, to tell her there's a flash flood warning in the Forksville area.

"I know, Mom," Nalin says.

"Are you gonna leave? You can drive to Maryand, stay with me for a few days."

"No, we're staying. We can move our stuff upstairs if we have to."

The phone connection is bad, and her mother's voice sounds crackly and wavering. She tells Nalin that she doesn't feel comfortable with her and Calvin living alone, so far from family. She says they need a dog.

Nalin chews on the phone cord. "What kind of dog?" Cal moves around the kitchen, picking up bills or old receipts and putting them down again. She wishes he would sit still.

"Get a greyhound," her mother says. "Get a greyhound, and you'll be blessed."

Nalin imagines a greyhound, thin, body shaped like a bow and tail tucked between its legs, cuddling with her in the bedroom as downstairs the kitchen table, the rocking chair, the unfinished Scrabble game, float in the floodwaters. She imagines the wooden-tile letters lifting from the board and drifting around the house, through the letter flap, down the street.

"Thanks, Mom."

"Of course, honey."

Nalin tries to remember what it was like to be young.

She remembers catching daddy long legs that she collected in jars, digging holes to China, an awkward first date chaperoned by her parents. As her mother hangs up, Nalin moves the curtain aside with her finger and looks into the rain. She never realized until now how the color of the river changes depending on the weather. Gray for snow. Blue for sun. Green for thunder. But brown, brown for rain, its ugliest color.

She met Cal the summer she graduated college. Early in their relationship, she liked to research cross-sections of the earth like they were maps and wondered if this is how he saw the world. In layers of soil, in cracks in the earth, in hidden pockets of air through which water traveled. In compounds that could ionize into minerals with worth.

They tried having a child once, when they were twenty-five. And a child grew, a little, blobby fetus that reminded Nalin of baby hamsters she'd seen. How strange it was that the fingers would eventually separate, that the tail of the fetus would split into legs. How strange it was that a body knew how to grow. She became more aware of the goblet-like curve of her uterus, that black void steadily, day-by-day, being filled. And she also knew when it became suddenly empty, when the life inside of her stopped.

Cal has moved out of the kitchen and into the living room. He's reading a newspaper, his legs propped up on the coffee table, his foot tapping to the beat of water on the trashcan outside.

When the drip in the bedroom still hasn't stopped, Nalin and Cal climb into the attic to find its source. They've spent the day replacing pots with plastic boxes, then boxes with trash pails, trying to contain the leak. But they're tired of the *ping* of water on water or water on pail. They're tired of dumping buckets of rain out the bathroom window. Cal carries a roll of duct tape, looped over his arm and nestled over his elbow. They stand with their feet apart, straddling the soft spaces between the beams. Nalin likes this part of the house, where the building's bones aren't masked by drywall and paint.

"We're inside the ribs," she says, and Cal shrugs.

They step from beam to beam, hands on the walls, feeling for wetness. There are only two boxes in the attic, the rest is bare. Nalin sifts through them as Cal touches his palms to the ceiling. She finds a dead light bulb, a journal, an empty photo frame, a dead cockroach which she flings into the corner.

"Here it is," Cal says in the corner. Nalin hears the crack of stretched duct tape.

She sits cross-legged on a beam, watching as he patches the house back together.

The rain gets heavier as the night goes on. Cal turns on his old police scanner, and lying in bed they listen to calls for help from neighborhoods downriver. Cal falls asleep as bridge closings are announced. Nalin turns down the volume and watches his sleeping form, tracing with her hand the dips and curves he creates in the comforter. "*Canyon State Park, bridge down.*" He looks so much smaller than he did when they met. She never thought she'd miss the belly, rounder than the palm of her hand, or the tree-trunk thighs of his thirties. But now that they've gone, age and inactivity hollowing him out, she misses them. She misses the space he took up. She misses how, in bed, no matter how close to the wall she lay, part of him was always touching her.

"Woman requesting help on High Street. Porch col-lapsing."

When Nalin was seventeen, she wrote letters in her journal to all the people she hadn't met yet. To her future daughter: *You'll like gardening. You won't like the color pink. You'll play soccer.* To her future husband: *You will be tall and warm and like swimming in creeks, never pools. You'll know how to catch catfish in the water with your bare hands and how to cook them over a fire. I'm sorry about the weird mole on my lower back. Also, for the snoring. I hope you'll learn to forget these things about me.*

She suddenly has the urge to do something surprising. To touch Cal in a way that makes him want her or miss her or hate her or love her. She presses her cheek to the concave between his shoulder blades. She slips her hand under his shirt, feeling for the heat of his skin. His skin is rough, slight-ly bumpy all over. Nalin touches his spine and then slides her hand to his stomach, feeling the hairs that grow around his bellybutton. She kisses the back of his neck, and when he's about to pull away, holds her lips there.

Cal grunts. He shifts in his sleep, pulling his body into the fetal position. Nalin wills herself to do more, to push further. But the moment has passed, and her husband's body doesn't feel like hers anymore, not something she can touch.

She dreams: The river splashes into her socks and makes whirlpools around her dress, which is strange, because she never wears dresses. Her husband is the size of a thumb, and he climbs between her bones, stands inside her ribcage, tick-les her from the inside.

. . .

112   the mother

In the morning, the rain is puddling again at the foot of Nalin and Cal's bed. Downstairs, they find that the basement has flooded, brown and muddy, boxes of cereal and apples floating around in it.

The house next door, built at the bottom of the bank and closest to the river, is submerged up to the back door. The kids, a young boy and a girl, have stuffed nose plugs up their nostrils and strapped raccoon-eye goggles over their faces and are cannon-balling off the roof of the gazebo. Nalin goes out back, umbrella in hand, and yells to their parents watching from the second story window if they need any help. They shake their heads, and Nalin stands at the edge of the porch, watching as the kids frog-stroke down and into the flood waters. Every time they emerge, they are holding something. A wiffle-ball. A garden hoe. They shout that they've found the lawn mower, seaweed knotted around the chain, and the birdbath, minnows swimming circles around the rim. The girl shrieks that she saw a dead cat, tail caught under a log. The boy says no, it's a rat. They dive again, come to the conclusion that it was their father's fleece jacket.

When Nalin goes back inside, Cal is running stuff up from the basement. Nalin finds a photo album, ink smudged under the plastic. As he retrieves boxes of slides and Christmas lights and files of geological maps, dripping puddles of muddy water onto the tiles, she flips through the album. Their trip to South Carolina, their tour of wine country, photos of her when her belly started to swell. All turned to rain in the running ink. Nalin pulls the pictures out of their plastic coverings and lays them out to dry.

The day passes, and they watch the river rise. They drink the last of the milk and heat cans of soup, which they eat with the end pieces of bread. All day, they watch things float by their house. Debris. Detached pieces of lives. Nalin spots a deer around noon, eyes rolling and tongue red, kicking against the current. She runs outside. She yells to Cal. There must be a way to save it. Grab the hose. The clothes line. Tie a lasso. But Cal just puts a hand on her shoulder. He says, "It'll be fine. Animals are better suited to nature than we are." Nalin saw the deer's wide-eyed look. She knows it has no hope. Cal stands there, immobile, and she wants to shout at him. She wants to shout at him to move, to try, to fight. Nalin takes a step toward the water, but the deer is being pulled and is already two houses away. Three houses. Now it's gone. Too far away to see its ears poking up above the waters.

She turns back to Cal. He's stepped out into the rain with her. He's looking up at the sky. She walks to the house. She shakes her head.

They spend the evening in the living room, listening to the sound of the basement filling with water, sloshing against the cinderblocks. Nalin worries the foundation will crumble, but Cal reassures her that the house was built strong. When the sun sinks behind the mountains, they don't turn on the lights, afraid of an electrical spark in the rising water. Instead, they go to the bedroom, light dusty candle stubs, and arrange flashlights on the dressers. They sit in silence on the carpet, watching the black mass of water slide by outside their reflections in the window. Nalin reaches for words to fill the silence, but can't stop thinking about all the lives the water carries with it. Their old clothes, saved from the damp closet, are still hanging over the headboard, and Nalin fingers the edge of a silver polyester jacket until Cal takes it from her. She turns to him, reaches for it out of instinct, but he wraps the jacket around his back and slips his arms through the sleeves. The sequined cuffs ride up past his bony wrists and the shoulders strain around his collarbones, leaving long shadows on the wall. Nalin watches as he takes one of her scarves, bright pink, covered in tiny, knit roses, and wraps it around his neck. Cal chuckles. Nalin suddenly realizes this is a game. Realizes she doesn't want it to stop.

Nalin wakes up the next morning to silence. Cal still sleeping, she slips out of bed and into the bathroom. She peers out the window. The river laps against the siding of the house, covering the porch and cutting off the trees at their bases. The sky is solid gray, and the water's surface is still.

She wakes Cal. "The rain's stopped."

They eat breakfast sitting on the counter. The flood has filled the basement and started leaking onto the first floor, covering the tiles with a brown film. Nalin moves around the house like she did as a child, jumping from the stairs to the sofa. From the sofa to the coffee table to the kitchen chairs. The ground is lava. Her home becomes a place without floors.

They eat handfuls of dry cereal out of the box. Then Cal suggests they take the canoe out to collect anything they can salvage from the back yard. The canoe is in the garage, and when they empty it and take it outside, Cal chooses the back seat, Nalin takes the center. As he propels them over the backyard, she curls her legs against her chest, listening to the water running against the sides of the boat, imagining she's in the belly of a whale. She props herself up on elbows, watching the little whirlpools stirred up by Cal's paddle. Together, they canoe over the vegetable garden, past sunflower faces and the tips of pine trees. They find Nalin's plastic garden gnome, her watering can. They find the neighbor's flowered dress, which had been hanging on the clothesline the day it rained, in knots around the fence. Cal reaches out with the paddle, pulls the dress into the canoe. "A gift," he says to Nalin. He smiles, the hollows in his cheeks filling. And so she takes it, fabric limp and dripping. She drapes it over her limbs, arranging it, erasing the places where her body can't fill the voids. Then, colored cotton tight around her arms, she leans her head back to rest on Cal's knees. She closes her eyes and imagines the dress fusing to her wrists and elbows like a second skin, curling, transforming her arms into fins.

My husband wasn't always a beam of light. Once, he had bones and guts. Once, he was a man with chronic heartburn and bad morning breath.

The doctors call it technological singularity. Your loved one's neuro-somethings are uploaded onto the data-web-stream-thinger. His body goes into a vegetative state, but his mind gets to transcend human intelligence and live infinitively as a thread of code and electricity traveling through the dimensions.

Just think of your husband as a beam of light, the doctors told me.

The day my husband transcended, I thought he was out grocery shopping. When he wasn't home by bedtime, I called the police, but they couldn't report him missing until he'd been gone for 24 hours. So I waited. I counted the hours. At hour 23, a package arrived, addressed to me. It contained a drive labeled "HUSBAND BACK-UP" and a glass plaque with his name etched across its surface. Underneath his name, the date of his transcendence followed by a dash and an infinity symbol.

I'm ashamed I didn't see this coming. My husband had always preferred tech to the physical. Pistons. Pixels. Processors. When we vacationed in Greenland to see the last of the great glaciers thunder down, he spent the trip behind his camera-phone. Our courtship took place mainly through emoticons. In person, he was stiff, he was awkward. But he could text eloquently.

Two of our friends had transcended already. Tom was uploaded after his heart attack last spring. Jessica transcended when they found the knuckle-sized pit of cancer in her uterus. Both emailed us from the data stream—long, single-sentence emails containing words we had to Google the meanings of.

My husband replied to every message, sent Tom and Jessica email after email with questions they never answered.

Give it a break, I told him.

And he replied, Aren't you the smallest bit curious? Everyone's greatest fear is death. Imagine never having to face that.

But didn't fear death. I'd always thought life was like a school field trip that you knew would just last a day, so you made the most of that day, and when it ended you couldn't be bitter because you knew the deal.

My husband said, That's an imperfect analogy.

And I said, It doesn't feel imperfect.

Now, I wait for what comes next. My husband's been a beam of light for three weeks. I check my inbox every half hour, waiting for a word from infinity.

If I could speak with him now, what would I say?

Maybe: What does a beam of light do all day?

Maybe: Have you been to space yet? Have you been in the belly of a whale?

I imagine him riding radio waves across Northern Russia and seismic rays to the earth's core. I imagine him forgetting what it's like to be ruled by three dimensions.

Maybe: Why didn't you tell me?

Maybe: I'll never follow you.

Maybe: Make a home inside my bones, buzz along my synapses. Convince me that your infinity is better.

When the apocalypse comes, we will stockpile our minds heavy with vine-ripe tomatoes, late-night text conversations with the boy who played second-chair clarinet, and the cool weight of a pearl necklace against our collarbones. We will stockpile our minds with wet football bleachers, the bone-like curve of the Xbox controller, and Butter's sandpaper-rough tongue, so that when our homes are overrun with flood waters, or zombies, or a flesh-eating virus, we will be able to leave these things behind.

When the apocalypse comes, we will not be afraid.

We will have our pepper spray, our parents' car keys that double as knives, and our Bic lighters.

We will tell ourselves that the dangers of the apocalypse are not so different from the dangers of our old lives. We were raised to avoid alleyways, to see every man as a potential danger, to walk at night in groups of three or more, to see death around every corner.

If apocalypse by flood, we will learn to fish with shoe strings and wads of gum. If by zombie, we will lock ourselves in the basement and be grateful our mothers kept canned foods in the cool, shelved corners. If by virus, we will run to the woods, to the mountain peaks we saw every morning on the horizon but never dared to climb.

When the apocalypse comes, we will realize: what a relief to give up our pre-apocalypse goals. Once the apocalypse is here, we won't care that we didn't get asked to slow dance at prom, or that we never retook the SATs. We won't care that we're waiting for an acceptance letter from Brown (and from our safety school). We will find comfort in the easy, obvious goals of survival: ensnare that fish, kill that zombie, find clean water.

When the apocalypse comes, we will stay with our families as long as we can, but we know it won't last. We will lose them in a late-night zombie raid, or to a great white wave, or maybe we will just take different exits when we reach the interstate.

We will forget our families, we will forget our crushes, we will forget our boyfriends' names. We will remember the strange things. We will remember how we borrowed our nameless boyfriends' socks in winter, how they slid down our ankles. We will remember Girl Scout cookies crumbled on tongues, hemp lanyards, and hand-sewn tote bags. We will remember how many things we used to make with our hands, but we won't remember when we stop remembering.

When the apocalypse comes, we will feel prepared in a way we have never felt before.

A month after we moved to Pforzheim, Germany, my husband came home with two baby Komodo dragons swaddled in his tweed work jacket. The size of kittens, scales soft, they looked like the newly-hatched alligators I'd seen in documentaries.

"For you," Philip said, basketing them into my arms. "Companions for when I'm away."

The dragons nipped at the ends of my sleeves with tiny, white teeth. I could feel their soft weight pressing against my chest as they squirmed in my arms.

"I got them from Letta, the chemistry teacher. We're allowed to keep them for two months, and then she's sending them to the zoo in Stuttgart."

He pulled a book out of his suitcase, *Caring for Your Reptile*. He read, "Reptiles are challenging, yet rewarding, pets that require regular attention."

The dragons' claws pricked through my wool sweater. Their muscles moved under their scales, which were as cool as stones. I wanted to drop the dragons, to push them away with my toe, to hide them under the couch. "Where will we keep them?" I asked.

Philip and I lived in a restored German farmhouse with a sloping roof and large attic but small rooms that held the heat and had us bumping into each other in doorways. Behind our house, the Black Forest was dark with pine and fir trees. Our closest neighbor was miles away. This was no place for lizards.

"We'll block them in the kitchen," Philip said. "I'll order crates for them to sleep in."

He scooped the dragons out of my arms and tipped them onto the tiled kitchen floor. They skittered, scattered, running for the shadowy spaces under the chairs. Philip went outside to the car and returned with a baby gate, which he placed in the doorway. The dragons growled against it, tested it with their teeth.

"They're completely legal under the Animal Regulation Act 4862," Philip said, seeing my uncertainty.

"They don't like the gate," I said. "Aren't Komodo Dragons vicious? What if they attack us in our sleep?"

Philip laughed and kissed me on the cheek.

That night, a storm roared. Philip didn't stir. He'd slung his arm over my shoulders in his sleep, pinning me to the bed, and I moved him carefully back under the blankets. I couldn't hear the dragons over the sound of the rain, and this made me nervous. The sky beyond our bedroom curtains was bruise-purple, and lightning struck once, twice, over the Forest. Philip's grandparents had once told me that the Black Forest contained all of the mammals that scientists believed were extinct. The Irish elk, the bilby, the Tasmanian tiger. The Black Forest hid all, and I imagined them now, recoiling against the thunder, finding shelter under roots.

When I woke the next morning, Philip was crouched on the kitchen floor, feeding the dragons cubes of leftover pork off the end of a toothpick. His hair was mussed with sleep, dark and prickly, in a way I'd found attractive when we first met.

I could see a sliver of skin where his shirt lifted up above his flannel pajama bottoms, exposing the scar from a childhood street hockey accident.

"*Guten Morgen,*" he said to me, and then again to the dragons. Good morning.

Over the past month, I'd taken to carrying an English-to-German dictionary around the house with me. I flipped through the pages. I spilled coffee over conjunctions. I tried to put new names to the objects I'd carried across the ocean with me.

I joined Philip on the floor. The dragons snarled at me, and Philip pushed them away with a swipe of his hand. I noticed teeth marks in the wood at the base of our table.

"Maybe we should keep them outside," I suggested.

Philip shook his head. I could smell dark coffee on his breath. "They'll learn to hunt if we leave them out. They'll go mean."

"Won't a cage make them meaner?" I asked, but he ignored me. He distracted the Komodos by placing food in front of their noses.

"*Aufwachen, drachen,*" I said. Wake up, dragons.

"Too harsh," Philip replied, not looking away from the dragons. "*Aufwachen.* It's a soft word."

Philip was raised by first-generation German immigrants in Brooklyn. When Philip was a child, his parents told him stories of their old country around the dinner table. Stories of the Krampus, a beast-man that stole misbehaving children from their beds, and of wolves that disguised themselves as people. "Nonsense," Philip called it. Like most children of immigrants, Philip's primary language became English once he started attending school. But his dreams remained in German. Sometimes I'd wake up to him muttering in his sleep, harsh consonants, soft umlauts.

When we married, Philip flew me to Germany for our honeymoon. I met Philip's grandparents, who spoke all the English words they knew, calling me *pretty girl,* asking, *how many babies?* "Not for a while," I'd laughed. We ate pot-roasted bratwurst and buttery bread rolls. Philip was three years older than me, quieter than me, mysterious. We walked in summer-warmed cattle fields. We went to pubs in Dusseldorf and danced polka with other couples. We were the happiest we'd ever be. So, four years later, when I made the mistake that bent our marriage, I was the one to suggest we return to Pforzheim.

"We'll be happier there," I told Philip. "It'll be our chance to restart, away from everything, back where we began. We'll visit the villages where your parents grew up, we'll go dancing."

Philip's grandparents had passed away a year ago, and I knew things would be different this time. Nevertheless, I hoped that Deutschland, with its magic forests and beast-men, could heal us.

The dragons swallowed the last of the pork, then scuttled to a patch of tiled sunlight. Philip sighed, stretched, rose to his feet. "Time for work," he said.

Philip taught sixth grade biology at the Buckenberg school for boys. He graded pop quizzes with a red pen at the dinner table every night.

He poured a to-go cup of coffee. I placed a hand on his back. I whispered, "*Aufwachen, aufwachen,*" more to myself than to him.

. . .

going mean

After Philip left, I let the dragons into the yard with me. I didn't trust them in the house alone. My husband was at work, the sun out, and I hung wet shirts and pants from the clothes line. As I rung the water out of pockets and seams, the dragons climbed onto each other's backs and rode each other like horses in the unmowed grass. They were too small to escape over the fence, and outside of the house like this, with the sun warming their scales, they seemed almost cute. I sat on the front stoop and watched them dinosaur-step over each other. It didn't seem possible, but already they looked bigger than they had the night before.

Four weeks in Germany, and I hadn't found a job. Back in America, in New Jersey, I'd managed a No-Kill Animal Shelter for dogs and cats. In my free time, I perused local pounds, looking for animals on the kill-list to bring back to my shelter. Feral cats, half-wild dogs that I'd give names to. Philip called me sentimental. He said I anthropomorphized animals, the most dangerous mistake a scientist could make.

Philip, at the time, taught middle school science. I raised a fuss every time he had his eighth grade science class dissect rats. He learned to stop telling me when it was dissection day, but I'd always smell the disinfectant on him, the latex on his hands.

Philip wanted children. He wanted to move back to Brooklyn and fill an apartment with babies. He wanted me with a child on my hip, another in my belly. I refused to have children until I had a stable career, until I'd traveled.

It was after one of our fights that I met Nico. Nico was the newest volunteer dog walker at the shelter. In his early-twenties, a few years younger than me, tan, born and raised in Venezuela. Not as muscular as Philip, but slim like a tree limb and with beautiful, dark hair he pulled back into a pony-tail.

After work one day, he invited me back to his apartment to see his collection of rescued pets, and I accepted. He lived close to the airport, under the Newark flight path. Jets roared overhead as he showed me his box turtle with the chipped shell living in his bathtub, his pygmy goat in his backyard, his three-legged Husky. Seeing him on his knees, forehead pressed against the dog's, melted something in me. I kissed Nico there on the floor, and he kissed me back. I'd never been with someone younger than me, someone who wasn't asking anything of me but the moment. The pygmy goat butted at the back screen door, the turtle scraped against the tiled floor. Once I started, I couldn't stop.

When it was over, I put my clothes on quickly. The exhilaration I'd felt minutes ago had vanished. I remembered Philip, in his fifth period right now, teaching sixth graders about cell mitosis, and was suddenly terrified by my attraction to Nico. It'd been so easy to cheat. For years I'd looked down on faithless husbands and disloyal wives with no idea that the potential to cheat had been inside me, too.

I left Nico, still reclined and bare-backed, on the tiled kitchen floor.

A week passed before I summoned up the courage to tell Philip.

"I understand if you want to leave me," I told him. We'd just finished dinner. Dirtied plates and an unfinished, bony turkey breast sat between us.

Philip left without a word and didn't come home that night. When he returned in the morning, he took my cellphone and threw it into the garbage disposal. I stood in the doorway and watched without trying to stop him. I heard the clunk of the phone landing against the blades.

After that, things seemed better. Philip tried to pick the parts of the phone out of the drain with tweezers. He told me, "You made a mistake, but it wasn't only your mistake. I take responsibility for not paying enough attention to you, for not recognizing your needs." He held my hands in his. He took off his glasses and placed them on the coffee table.

In bed that night, he told me his grandparents had split up for a short time before he was born. His oma moved to Prague, his opa to Brunswick, and it took only four months for them to realize they'd made a mistake and return to each other. I reached for Philip under the blankets, but he twitched away from me.

"This will take time," he said. "I haven't forgiven you yet."

In my backyard in Pforzheim, the dragons circled the perimeter of the yard, rubbing their black and yellow scales against the fence, looking for a weak section. As I watched, I coiled grass around my fingers. The dragons licked the air, and I smelled the air. It was late summer, the air that flowed out of the Black Forest was cold and dark.

When the dragons reached the back of the yard, they started to fight over something in the grass. They shouldered each other and dug into the soil with their front claws. I watched, mesmerized, as one of the dragons tensed. The other backed off as its brother dug its feet into the lawn and pulled. An earthworm, the longest I'd ever seen, nearly two feet, snapped out of the soil and hung, swinging, from the dragon's jaws. I stood, but before I could reach them, the dragon had slung the worm up into the air, swallowed it whole.

…

Every day, Philip came home from school with a set of dragon facts. "Did you know baby Komodo dragons spend their first few years in the trees?" "Komodos see the world like a snake does, by tasting molecules in the air." "Male Komodos engage in ritualistic combat for their female mates, wrestling in an upright position, sometimes fighting to the death."

The weekend came, and he read from the reptile book, "Your lizard will molt several times during its first months of life. Help it along with regular scrubbing."

He filled the upstairs bathtub with hot water and asked me to bring the dragons upstairs.

I hadn't touched the Komodos since they ate the worm. I'd seen dogs and cats attack each other or stalk mice at the shelter, but with them there was always an element of play in the fight. There was always hesitation before the kill. The dragons' approach had been unapologetic, and I didn't know what to make of it.

I herded the dragons upstairs with the end of a broom. They didn't resist, eager to explore a new section of the house. In the bathroom, Philip lifted them by their chests and dropped them, one at a time, into the full bathtub. They dog-paddled in the water and clawed at the smooth sides of the tub.

I stood in the doorway as Philip scrubbed them down. With a toothbrush, he brushed at the space around their eyes. He cooed to the dragons, rubbing their bellies with bars of soap.

"What are you going to name them?" he asked me.

I looked at the dragons, but no names came to mind. "I'm still deciding."

going mean

The dragons kicked suds up onto Philip's T-shirt. One of them twisted in the water, nipped at its brother.

"*Nicht*," Philip said, flicking the dragon on the nose.

The dragon turned on him. It coiled under his hand and sunk its teeth into Philip's ring finger. Blood bloomed in the water.

"Damn it," Philip said. He jumped to his feet, cradled his finger. His first dragon-injury. "I'm okay, I'm okay. Just watch them."

He left the room, dripping blood onto the floor behind him. I listened to his feet hit the steps. The dragons were back to paddling circles in the tub. So serene now, all their aggression spilled out. I sat on the toilet and watched them.

Philip returned with his finger wrapped in gauze.

"You should get stitches," I said. I realized now that I should be helping him, comforting.

"What do you care?" Philip snapped. He took a deep breath. I could see blood pooling under the white gauze. "I'm sorry. I didn't mean it. Maybe I'll stop by the doctor before work tomorrow."

I helped him empty the tub, scrubbing the blood from the rim of the drain. We lifted the dragons onto the toweled floor. They were heavier than I expected, nearly the size of beagles.

As Philip changed into dry clothes, I sat on our bed and Googled *komodo dragons* on my laptop. I learned that they originated in Indonesia, where they'd swim from island to island searching for mates. I learned that adult Komodos can grow up to ten feet long and weigh 200 pounds. Adult dragon saliva teems with over 50 strains of bacteria that can kill a bitten animal within 24 hours.

I shared this information with Philip.

"It was just an accident," he said. "They haven't been trained yet, but they will be soon. You can train reptiles like dogs. And we'll give them back before they're too big."

Philip crawled under the covers next to me, and I closed my laptop. I took Philip's hand in mine. His injured finger had swollen, the knuckle almost the size of a grape. I felt bad for not helping him when the dragon lashed out. Since my one night stand, Philip and I had been intimate only rarely, and seeing him in pain reminded me of why we'd moved to Germany.

The bedroom window was open, and I could smell the Forest, hear branches brushing against branches. I kissed Philip's knuckle. I slung my arm around his waist and kissed the peak of his shoulder. At first, I thought he might already be asleep, but after a moment, Philip rolled over and embraced me under the blankets. He kissed my neck, and I bit into his shoulder. A quick, hard bite to the shoulder blade.

Philip recoiled. "What was that?"

He pulled away from me, and I pulled the blankets up over my chest.

"I'm sorry."

"Maybe we should talk," Philip said. "Is that what you want?"

I was silent. I felt like a reprimanded pet.

Philip started talking. He told me that he had started a science club at school, he told me that he and Letta were planning a joint field trip to the city science museum next month. I tuned him out. I was confused by what had driven me to bite him. I was confused by the spontaneity of it. I could still taste the saltiness of Philip's skin in my mouth. I realized I wanted to bite into his shoulder and not let go. To see him run into the yard, shoeless, and howl at the Forest.

When Philip fell asleep, I reached over him for his reptile book, which was sitting closed on his nightstand. I took it into the bathroom to read under the light. The pages fell open on the Komodo dragon chapter, and I read, "Indonesian legend claims the dragon as natives' kin. Modern villagers still see the Komodo dragon as an ancestor."

I thought of the dragons stalking insects under the couch. Or waiting by the foot of the stairs. Their thoughts so far from human.

Philip spent the rest of the weekend dangling cat food in front of the dragons' noses, trying to train them to use a litter box. The harder he tried, the more the dragons rebelled. On Sunday morning, they knocked over the baby gate and rampaged through the house while we were still in bed. We woke up to Philip's lesson plans scattered over the living room floor in snow-like shreds. The rocking chair legs were splintered with teeth marks. The dragons were nowhere to be seen.

"Tap into your lizard brain," Philip told me.

We searched the house together.

I found the first dragon, curled in the hallway closet, tail coiled around the handle of Philip's briefcase. He found the second hiding between the folds of the living room curtains.

I could feel the dragons' tension growing and was relieved when he left for work on Monday. I wanted to try something.

I heard the car clear the driveway, and I stepped into the kitchen, now barricaded with chairs. The dragons were sprawled in a patch of sunlight, and they didn't move when I approached them. They looked thinner than they should be. Their skin was leathery, too big for their bodies. It draped over their shoulder blades, hung under their chins.

I sat next to the closest Komodo, cross-legged.

"*Gute drachen*," I said.

I leaned back and turned until, like the Komodos, I was sprawled on my stomach across the tiled floor. I reached slowly, touched the dragon's side. The scales felt like chain mail. The dragon's eyelids flickered. I could see my reflection in its black pupil. I expected it to twist, to bite me like it had Philip, but instead it flicked its tongue. Nudged me with its scaly nose.

I inched away, my heart pounding. The dragons recognized something in me, something they didn't recognize in Philip. I was afraid of what that might be.

"*Was ist das?*" I asked the dragons. What is it?

That night I told Philip I wanted to go into town the next day.

"I just need to get out," I told him, and he seemed pleased. He looked up from his grading.

"You can meet me for lunch," he said. "We'll meet at *coffee boxx*."

For dinner, he made schupfnudel, rolled noodles over sauerkraut. He hummed as he cooked, and warm steam filled the kitchen. The dragons watched with their noses tipped into the air. The meal was bland. I itched to pour salt over it, or pepper, but didn't want to insult him.

"My grandparents' recipe," he told me. "True German cuisine."

The dragons licked at his ankles, tasted the air.

At noon the next day, I shepherded the Komodos into the kitchen. They looked at me with coal-like, betrayed eyes, but I ignored them. As I climbed into the car, I realized I'd forgotten my translation book. I thought about going back for it, but decided I wouldn't need it. I could learn German the old-fashioned way, through experience. I could make my way through the world by reading emotions and inflections instead of words.

For the first ten minutes of the drive into town, the Black Forest streamed by the window, dark and dense and earthy. The steering wheel hummed under my palms. A dirt road turned off the pavement and vanished into the pines. For a moment I thought I might take it, give in to the sweet, quiet pull of the Forest. Drive until the wheels were muddy, until the car looked more animal than machine.

I forced myself to keep going. The Forest gave way to city. Geometric, red-roofed buildings, carefully sculptured trees. I drove slowly, unsure of the rules here.

The café was small with salt-streaked windows and tight booths. Black and white photos of cityscapes hung on the walls. I ordered at the counter, "*Darf ich einen Kaffee*," proud of myself for remembering the words. May I have a coffee?

I spotted Philip in the back of the café, and he waved me over. A woman sat in the booth next to him.

"Sweetie, this is Letta," Philip said as I approached.

I slid into the booth across from them.

"How are the dragons?" Letta asked, smiling. There were spaces between her teeth, and I could tell by her tight-lipped smile that they embarrassed her. She wore khakis and a buttoned-up shirt. A careful pony-tail. I imagined her teaching chemistry classes, mixing perfect solutions in lab beakers, showing twelve-year old boys how to create controlled chemical fires. All the boys love her. She never sweats in her lab coat. She doesn't hold pop quizzes. She is kind, even to the boys who don't participate.

"Letta and I were just having a work meeting," Philip explained, reaching across the table to touch my arm. "Discussing the problem *mit privaten Bildungseinrichtungen.*"

"The problems with educational institutions," Letta translated. "I was just leaving, I don't want to interrupt."

Philip put a hand on her shoulder. "Oh no, stay. We don't mind."

I watched how Philip's hand lingered, and wondered if it was for me to see.

Letta settled back into the booth. "How brave of you to fly to Germany with your husband," she said. "Germany is so fast."

"She's learning the language quickly," Philip said. "Show her, hun."

I cupped the hot base of the coffee mug in my palms. "Um. *Die Drachen sind. Sind in Ordnung.*"

"Dee-dra-ha-hen," Philip corrected.

"Great, such good enunciation," Letta said.

I sipped my coffee. It blossomed hot and dark on my tongue.

"She'll be a true German soon enough," Philip said.

I turned to Letta. "You grew up here. What do you know about the Black Forest?"

"Oh, I don't go into the Forest," Letta said. She dabbed at her mouth with a napkin, then folded it into a triangle. "My family has a story about my great-grandpapa. He was a craftsman, a woodworker. One day he went into the Forest to do his work, and he never came back. My mother says he was eaten by a beast-man. Silly, I know, but I can't break tradition."

Philip laughed, and as he laughed his pinky touched Letta's forearm. I watched the ease with which he touched her and waited for the jealousy to rise. I was surprised when it didn't. Watching Philip interact with Letta, I felt nothing. All I felt was a need to return to the edge of the Forest, to return to my dragons.

"Maybe your grandpapa ran away," I said. "Maybe he wanted to leave."

Philip glared at me, but I felt none of it.

"Excuse me," I said, and stood.

I walked out of the café, didn't look back. I got in the car. As I merged onto the highway, I passed a sign for Prague. I thought, I could slip over country lines. I could let Europe unfold beneath me.

Philip and I were silent for most of the evening. I could tell he thought I'd been rude, but I didn't want to fight. I was tired of the tension between us.

After dinner, he told me, "Do you know why German words are so long? *Lebensabschnittpartner*, for example. It means, the person I am with today. In America we would simplify it and say 'partner' or 'date.' But here, we understand that nothing can be erased, so we let our words build."

I didn't respond. Sitting on the floor, I played tug-of-war with the dragons and a piece of jerky.

A small, brown mouse skittered across the kitchen

floor, and in a flash the dragons had forgotten the jerky.

"Grab them," said Philip. He stood, reached for one of the dragon's tails, but it slipped out of his grasp.

The dragons skidded across the tiles. The mouse cornered itself between the oven and cabinets. One of the Komodos pinned it with a claw.

I sat, watching, as Philip swung at the dragons with a broom.

"Help me," he said, and I shook my head.

I heard a small click as the mouse's spine broke under a Komodo's claw. The dragon swallowed the body.

Philip sat back down, put his face in his hands. "They won't always be like this," he said. "They'll get better."

"Letta is going to send them to the zoo," I said.

"Not yet."

Philip went upstairs to shower. A few strands of mouse fur lay in the corner of the room, and I swept them into a dustpan. The dragons orbited my ankles. When I didn't give them attention, they scrambled to the backdoor and scratched at the wood.

"You don't want to go out there," I said, but they kept scratching.

I thought of something Nico had told me, before we'd kissed on the floor, when our relationship was still simple and guiltless, and for the first time in a while I allowed myself to think of him.

It was his first day volunteering at the shelter. I'd just brought in a wild Doberman I'd found rooting around a dumpster in the city. It growled at other dogs until I gave it its own kennel. It wouldn't eat the dog food I poured into its bowl. Its eyes went wild when I slid a muzzle over its jowls.

"No one's going to adopt him," Nico said, watching me struggle to calm the dog. "He'll never be happy in a house. He would have been better off left alone."

I remember looking up at Nico, the end of his pony-tail tucked inside the collar of his shirt, and not believing him.

I tipped the mouse fur out of the dust pan and into the garbage.

Philip called down the stairs, his voice faint over the sound of the shower, "I invited Letta over for dinner tomorrow. I think you guys could really hit it off."

The dragons scratched at the door with urgency. They were leaving shallow scars in the wood, and I pushed them away with the side of my foot.

One day the Komodo dragons would be as big as I am. One day they'd tear apart an animal larger than a rodent. It wouldn't matter to them if they were in a zoo or in our house. It wouldn't matter that Philip and I had cared for them. They'd experienced violence and couldn't forget it.

I listened to the water traveling through the walls of the house, up to Philip, who would be coming downstairs soon to tell me about his lesson plans, to correct me on my pronunciation, to make me feel guilty about the mistakes I made.

The dragons returned to the door like magnets to metal. This time I opened it for them. I stood in the doorway and watched them skitter off into the dark grass. Their skin looked ocean-gray in the starlight, loose around their shoulders and ready to molt. Their noses tipped into the wind like overturned wine glasses.

The water stopped.

I put on shoes and walked out into the yard. The grass was wet on my ankles.

"What do you want?" I asked the dragons.

They licked the air, smelling for me, and I knew their answer. The dragons wanted to stomp into the forest. They wanted to grow large there, larger than their brothers and sisters in Indonesia. Winter was coming, but they would dig holes with their strong claws, bury their plated bodies under the soil and let their blood turn to stone until spring came again. They were dragons, full of muscle and sinew, and they wanted better than comfort. They wanted wild.

"Sweetie?" I heard Philip's voice faintly, traveling down the stairs.

I walked to the edge of the yard, the dragons at my heels. I knocked down the decorative fence with the bottom of my foot, and the dragons claw-climbed over it. Together, we approached the dark line of trees. Together, we faced the place where all the forgotten beasts hide.

going mean

acknowledgments

This book is a product of so many people and places. First and foremost, thank you to my parents and brother, who took me on adventures in the woods and taught me to see the earth as a place to be protected and explored. Thank you for giving me the belief that I can achieve anything.

To my teachers, Gary Fincke, Catherine Zobal Dent, Silas Dent Zobal, Joseph Scapellato, Karla Kelsey, Glen Retief, Tom Bailey, Randy Robertson, Dan Mayer, Matt Bell, Peter Turchi, Tara Ison, Melissa Pritchard, and Mike McNally: thank you for teaching me to create and write bravely.

Thank you to the Writers House and my friends who belong with it, for your sense of humor and your support and your love of games with made-up titles.

Thank you to my housemates on Broadmor (and their animals), to the Write Wednesday crew, and to my colleagues and friends at ASU who saw this book in its earliest stages. Special thanks to the amazing Sam Martone, MFA buddy and one of this manuscript's first readers.

To Casey, Tait, and Rachel: thank you for your love, for the snowy camping trips, and for the icy swims at Worlds End under bat-infested skies.

Thank you, Will, for being a voice I trust and a source of so many good things. Your way of seeing the world inspires and challenges me in the best ways. Thank you for the title.

Thank you to the Susquehanna University Writers' Institute, the Arizona State University MFA in Creative Writing, the Virginia G. Piper Center for Creative Writing, the National University of Singapore, the University of Stirling in Scotland, the Rutgers University Camden Summer Writers' Conference, and the Port Townshend Writers' Conference.

And finally, thank you to the journals that gave these stories homes first, in slightly different forms: "We Know More" in *PANK*, "Astronauts" in *Hobart*, "Swallowed" in *SmokeLong Quarterly*, "Swarm" in *Booth*, "Animal Skin" in *Passages North Online*, "Closer" in *North American Review*, "Stones" and "Another Time" in *Sundog Lit*, "To Date a Time Traveler" in *Sonora Review*, "The Mother" in Swarm, "A Place Without Floors" in *Salamander*, "Once He Was a Man" in *Threadcount*, "Girls Prepare for the Apocalypse" in *New South*, and "Going Mean" in *Yemassee*.

Dana Diehl is a graduate of the Susquehanna University Writers Institute and earned her MFA in Fiction at Arizona State University. Her stories have appeared in *North American Review, Passages North, Booth*, and elsewhere. She lives in the Sonoran Desert of Arizona.

Jellyfish Highway Press is postindustrial bioluminescence; we're abyssal gigantism.

Jellyfish Highway Press
www.jellyfishhighway.com
Atlanta, GA

CPSIA information can be obtained
at www.ICGtesting.com
Printed in the USA
BVOW06s1151230217
477007BV00008B/32/P